The Indians Won

Native Edge
David Heska Wanbli Weiden, Series Editor

Native Edge will highlight established and emerging Native voices producing experimental and genre work in fiction and creative nonfiction: mystery, horror, science fiction, and noir sitting side by side with experimental literary fiction and creative nonfiction. Intended for general readers and classroom use, these books will offer compelling original work bearing on the Native experience in North America and worldwide, and the series will also explore past works that may have gone underappreciated in their day and are now judged to be ripe for revival.

Also available in the Native Edge series:

The Strangers: A Novel by Katherena Vermette

NATIVE
EDGE

The Indians Won

Martin Cruz Smith

University of New Mexico Press
Albuquerque

University of New Mexico Press edition published
2024 by arrangement with the author
Printed in the United States of America

ISBN 978-0-8263-6604-7 (paper)
ISBN 978-0-8263-6605-4 (ePub)

Library of Congress Cataloging-in-Publication data
is on file with the Library of Congress.

Founded in 1889, the University of New
Mexico sits on the traditional homelands of the
Pueblo of Sandia. The original peoples of New
Mexico—Pueblo, Navajo, and Apache—since time
immemorial have deep connections to the land
and have made significant contributions to the
broader community statewide. We honor the land
itself and those who remain stewards of this land
throughout the generations and also acknowledge
our committed relationship to Indigenous peoples.
We gratefully recognize our history.

Cover photograph by Nik Shuliahin via Upsplash
Designed by Isaac Morris
Composed in Pilsner and Utopia

For Em and in memory of Robert Riggs

Contents

Foreword

Let me just say it up front: *The Indians Won* is a groundbreaking work of Native American fiction and deserves to be included in the canon of Indigenous literature. The novel is apparently the first alternate history to be written by a Native author, though others would take up the form in years to come. The book is enormously entertaining to read, but there's a deeper message within its pages. *The Indians Won* presents a unique vision of Indigenous sovereignty and identity, one that's even more important today than when it was published.

I imagine many readers are surprised by the description of Martin Cruz Smith, bestselling author and Mystery Writers of America Grand Master, as a Native American writer. I'll admit that I was as well, as Smith is not usually included in discussions of major Indigenous authors. But Martin Cruz Smith is Pueblo, as noted in the first edition of the novel;[1] his mother, Louise Smith, was a jazz singer later known for her work in support of Native American rights. I discovered this fact in the early 2010s, when I was doing thesis research for my MFA degree at the Institute of American Indian Arts in Santa Fe. That thesis was an attempt to trace the first Native American crime writers, and my work led me to Smith's novel *Nightwing*,[2] arguably the first thriller written by an Indigenous author. I'd long been a fan of Smith's Arkady Renko novels, including the wildly successful *Gorky Park*, and I was astounded to discover that Smith is, in fact, Native American. Delving more deeply into Smith's books, I found references to his first published novel, *The Indians Won*, long out of print and difficult to find in the rare book marketplace.

After several weeks of searching, I was able to locate a battered copy of the original Belmont Books paperback edition, which listed the author as "Martin Smith" and noted that he was twenty-seven years old, a recent graduate of the University of Pennsylvania, and lived in New York with his wife and small daughter. I later learned that Smith added his maternal grandmother's maiden name, Cruz, in the 1970s in order to distinguish himself from the other Martin Smiths who were writing at the time. I was (and still am) impressed by the fact that Smith wrote the novel just several years out of college, and while raising a family and working in journalism. What I found in the yellowed and frayed pages of my copy of *The Indians Won* surprised me.

The novel is divided into two alternating timelines. The first, set in the mid-1800s, imagines a world in which the great leader Crazy Horse had not been assassinated and instead worked, along with the fictional character John Setter (also known as Where The Sun Goes), to unite all of the Native nations in North America. Backed by weapons supplied by European powers, the unified Natives defeat the American forces and establish a pan-Indian nation in the middle of the continent. The narrative is filled with historical figures such as Sitting Bull, Geronimo, Red Cloud, and Wovoka, and it details their actions in the alternative universe wherein the Natives were able to defeat the colonizers and retain their freedom and land. The second timeline envisions the same country, known as the Indian Nation, in the 1970s. The nation, now well established and governed by Indigenous principles, is a nuclear power and engaged in a cold war with the United States, which exists only on the coasts.

My favorite sections of the novel are Smith's vivid descriptions of the battles between the American and Indian forces in the first timeline. We see famous American generals completely overwhelmed by the military strategies employed by Indigenous leaders, primarily Crazy Horse. For the Native reader, these passages are, of course, incredibly satisfying. I found myself pumping my fist and actually cheering while reading these chapters.

But the machinations and maneuvers of these well-known Natives in their battles to create their own country reveals something else: a vision of how a pan-Indian nation would have come into being, and how such an Indigenous state would have differed from the Western capitalistic system that ultimately prevailed. It's tempting to focus on the book's descriptions of Native forces overwhelming the American army, but—in my opinion—the enduring value of the book lies in its conception of Indigenous governance, culture, and ideals of the Indian Nation, the fictional state formed after the defeat of the American forces.

I'll argue that *The Indians Won* not only depicts what might have been historically, but *what still could be*. That is, the novel envisions a world in which Indigenous principles are used to benefit and unite Native peoples in a way that's radically different than in Western democracies. In the twentieth-century timeline, the Indian Nation stays neutral in World War II, declines to join the United Nations, disavows economic and political expansionism, and remains true to traditional Native values. There are no banks, because "the idea of hoarding money was repugnant."[3] Foreign trade is discouraged, and factories create goods only for Native citizens. Yet this rejection of modern capitalism serves the Indian Nation well. "It had no wars since its liberation, no mass depressions economically or spiritually, never shown signs of intellectual discontent."[4]

Smith's historical reimagining depicts how a traditionally communitarian political system might have operated and provides a roadmap of sorts for Native communities in the twenty-first century, one in which Indigenous citizens work together for common goals.[5] Collective resistance and activism—from Alcatraz to Standing Rock—has remained an important part of the struggle for Indigenous rights, and these movements are likely to continue. *The Indians Won* provides an alternative vision for a Native future, one in which Indigenous values are central for intergenerational self-determination, liberty, and equality.

In the end, *The Indians Won* is a great read by one of the masters of modern fiction. I believe the time is right to introduce this wonderful book to a new generation, one that will enjoy it and embrace its lessons as we continue the struggle for sovereignty and justice around the world.

—David Heska Wanbli Weiden, Native Edge Series Editor

Notes

1. Martin Smith, *The Indians Won* (New York: Belmont Productions, 1970).
2. Martin Cruz Smith, *Nightwing* (New York: W. W. Norton & Co., 1977).
3. Smith, *The Indians Won*, 201.
4. Smith, *The Indians Won*, 205.
5. I acknowledge my debt to an excellent scholarly article by Sara Spurgeon and recommend it to those interested in further commentary on the novel. Sara Spurgeon, "'The Bomb Was like the Indians': Trickster Mimetics and Native Sovereignty in Martin Cruz Smith's *The Indians Won*," *American Quarterly*, 66, no. 4 (2014): 999–1020.

The Indians Won

Prologue

In the chateau of Azay le Rideau, in the summer of 1875, a private conference was being held between representatives of five nations. These men had met during the past five years to discuss international monetary affairs. They did not represent their countries so much as they represented countries within countries; that is, the sources of power behind a nation's power.

The topic of discussion was investment. All had experience in individual investment, especially in Africa. This they cared to refer to as primitive finance. The next step, made in twos and threes, finally achieving a sort of concert, had been in China. This entente found that dividing the spoils beforehand was a more efficient manner of colonization and reduced friction between themselves. They were among the most advanced thinkers of their time.

As their carriages drove along the Loire, they expanded their thoughts into that land between fantasy and profit. When a man named John Setter came to talk to them, he found them naturally receptive. They had considered America before, the land they had left such a short time before.

During the Civil War in the United States, they succeeded

in having the Confederacy named a "belligerent" and liable to international acknowledgement. They welcomed Confederate agents in London and Paris and bought fifteen million dollars in Confederate bonds. They built warships for the Confederacy and the English government took them past the Union blockade. Sympathy for the Confederacy in European upper-class circles was overt.

In 1861, Emperor Napoleon III sponsored a coalition by the states of Europe for intervention. The Czar refused to join and the first coalition died. A second coalition was proposed in 1862. Part of Queen Victoria's cabinet voted in favor of it but it was decided to wait another year. A third coalition arose in 1863 with general agreement between the parties that a statement would be made recognizing the Confederacy. Lee, on his way to Philadelphia, was stopped at Gettysburg and the Confederate Armies retreated. There were no more coalitions for intervention. One battle had ended their speculation.

There were other investments, though. A poor one by Louis Napoleon on his own in Mexico, installing the doomed Maximilian. More cautious ones followed the end of the war. The Credit Mobilier financed construction of railroad lines into the Indian Territories with just a little less return than it got from its Chinese investment, taking forty-four million dollars from the Union Pacific venture after bribing a member of the United States Congress to serve as president and persuading the vice president to do its lobbying. They were not completely unaware of the wealth to be made in developing nations.

The representative of the English houses, for example, had visited Canada, the north country that the Americans were always implying would soon fall into their hands. Canada had been invaded twice in vain by the ambitious Yankees, and now the vast English monopoly on the Far West fur trade was being challenged. The logic of the Americans seemed to be that since they owned Washington and Alaska, they should have everything in between, too.

The Frenchman, the host, was offended by the slight France had received in the execution of Maximilian. His friend Jules Ferry demanded a return to *la gloire*, but bad news was being received from Hanoi where the French Annamese empire was shaken by the Black Flag guerrillas. His hopes were encouraged by the German representative, an appreciator of the local Vouvray. The German followed his chancellor's policy of diverting French energies into colonial concerns to take their minds off the fact that they had lost Alsace and Lorraine to Germany during the 1870 war.

The other two representatives were less passionate about new speculations. The Russian came along mostly to be sure that nothing was said behind his back about Asia. In regard to the rest of the world, he was most idealistic. Before he went to sleep each night, his lips made out the words "Trans-Siberian Railroad." The Belgian representative was pure good humor. Belgium, a small nation, sat on the Congo while its missionaries surveyed a railroad line across the interior of China. There were profits enough for all, he said. Let us be friends.

They all agreed that it would be enjoyable to see the United States humiliated in some fashion but that they did not see how the humiliation might occur. The possibility that Setter suggested, an Indian Nation cutting the United States in half, was so unlikely as to be ridiculous. Certainly, if the Indians could come together and achieve some sort of military stability and demanded only equipage in return for contracts to the last great source of natural wealth in the world, they would be interested.

But everyone knew that Indians couldn't stick together.

Chapter One

Nothing lives long,
Except the earth and the mountains

—White Antelope

A few feet above the grass hung a flat layer of blue-grey smoke. It seemed to cut in half the warriors who walked through it. Below, out of danger from the smoke, were the bodies of the soldiers, naked and white and red where trophies had been taken.

The bodies stretched through a depression over the prairies and on up to a hill. It was on a retreat to the hill that most of them had died. There were two hundred *Wasichu*, white men, sprawled among their dead horses, their belts and caps. All of their Springfields had been taken. They had come to the Greasy Grass along the Little Big Horn to herd the people they called Sioux back to their fort. They had also come for revenge.

Twice, already, the army under Generals Crook and Terry had been thrown back by the Lakota, as the Sioux called themselves. Crook had almost lost the Seventh Cavalry at the Battle of the Rosebud. Only a charge by his Shoshone scouts under Chief Washakie had saved him from disaster. It was the job of General Custer to fix the Lakota in one place and hold them until Terry arrived.

Even as they left the safety of their fort, the song "Garryowen" beating jig time, the Seventh Cavalry was expected. Sitting Bull hung from the sacred tree of the Sun Dance until his breasts were torn out and he achieved a vision. Hundreds of soldiers were falling upside down onto the Greasy Grass. He would not be able to fight but he would be able to say that the attack by Reno was only a feint to divert the Indian defense.

When Custer drew up his horses to charge through the camp, as he had charged so well throughout the Civil War and through undefended Indian villages since, he gave the order to dismount instead. In front and on his flanks were the Lakota, the Tsitsistas, Inuna-Ina (Arapaho), their councils of San Arc, Oglala, Uncpapa, Yankton, Santee, and Brule. In front, their bonnets quivering in the air, were the great chiefs Gall, White Shield, White Bull, and Big Road of the Lakota; Wolf That Has No Sense, Yellow Nose, and Two Moons of the Tsitsistas; and in front of all, Tashunka Witko, They Fear His Horses, the chief they called Crazy Horse. There were fifteen thousand Indians in all.

It took little more than an hour. Pte-san-hunka, White Bull, twenty-six years old, had only been bruised by a bullet. *He* knelt over a body, stripping it. His friend Bad Soup staggered over with the exhilaration of the fight and asked whether White Bull wanted the scalp. White Bull said that the hair was too short, although the struggle had been hard. The Wasichu had shot at him, had clubbed him with a rifle and then tried to bite his nose off.

"Look at him," Bad Soup said. "*Pehin hanska*, Long Hair, thought he was the greatest man in the world. Now he is there."

White Bull stood up and displayed a matched pair of pearl-handled pistols. When the pistols were brought to They Fear His Horses, riders were sent out to agencies in the West, the South, and north to the Siksika, the Blackfeet. Two riders were sent with a small herd of ponies for relays to the Canadian border.

On July 6, the news had reached the East. In a ladder of descending headlines, the *New York World* said: "Custer Killed—Disastrous Defeat of the American Troops by the Indians—Slaughter of Our Best and Bravest—Grant's Indian Policy Come to Fruit—A Whole Family of Heroes Swept Away—Three Hundred and Fifteen American Soldiers Killed and Thirty-One Wounded." The policy derided was the new one of concentration, a change from the previous one of extermination. General Sheridan was placed in charge of ending the insurrection that had defeated two armies and liquidated a third. Orders were sent from Washington via St. Louis that as the Indians broke their vast camp and divided for fresh food for the winter, Crook and Terry should follow them and wipe them out one by one.

Along the Canadian border, the Siksika were not roaming in small families as usual. For years their hunting parties had been smaller and smaller, just as the buffalo herds had been smaller and smaller. In antelope shirts almost pure white, in bright leggings made of Hudson's Bay Company blankets, the tall Siksika, the ones called Blackfeet, were coming together instead. The eight bands of the North Siksika, the fifteen bands of the Bloods, the twenty-five bands of the Piegan were all coming together and heading south over the Sweetgrass Country. By the times they assembled in Montana Territory, Big Lake would count six thousand of his people.

Tu-ukumah, Black Horse, was chief of the Comanche, the nation of horsemen who every year rode as far down as Durango to rob the Mexicans. Operating as companies, they brought hundreds of slaves back to perform the drudgery of their camps. Now they were leaving the slaves, as the bands moved in the night from Fort Sill, the herds of ponies like shadows, the noses of the stallions covered by hands to keep them silent: the Detsanaguka (Wanderers) and their chief Quanah Parker, the northern Yapa called Root Eaters, the daring Kotsoteka (Buffalo Eaters) and the largest of the bands, the fanatic Penateka (Honey Eaters). Leading the columns away from Oklahoma Territory were the Kwakari (Antelopes), at the head of a host two thousand strong. The dust of twenty thousand horses rose in the dark.

In the west, there were a few more minutes of daylight. The setting sun lit up a rolling sea of sunflowers. The sunflowers were winter fodders for the Utes and yellow dye for their clothes. Ground up it served as *poezhuta sapa*, coffee. and as cures for their diseases. The flowers stained the feet of the families as the two chiefs of the Ute, Omay, Arrow, of the northern people and Ignacio of the southern bands, met. A yellow sea waved in farewell.

White Sun Rising was dead six years in the Nevada Sierra. His nation, the Paiute, lived on strips of sage prairie bounded by giant mountains whose caps were always lined with snow. His son, Wovoka, The Cutter, was the new Prophet. Twenty years old, he was a preacher of his father's revelation—the resurrection of the Indian. The stolid, muscular Paiutes, drawn by the vision, were leaving their farms and hovels in the Nevada valleys and joining their Prophet as his vision spread out. Their friends the Banakwut, Bannock, led by Buffalo Horn, would meet them at Utah Territory.

General Oliver Howard was on the move, too. His assignment was to move the Nimipu, Nez Percé. to the Lapwai reservation. He had seven hundred soldiers of the First Cavalry to do the job. Since the chief Old Joseph had died it shouldn't be too hard, even though the chief's last words to his son were, "This country holds your father's body. Never sell the bones of your father and mother." In-mut-too-yah-lat-la, Thunder Going Over the Mountains, listened.

The Modoc did not have to listen. When they were taken to their reservation three years before, fifty of them had broken away and into the Oregon Lava Beds. There they held off twelve hundred soldiers for weeks. When they came down for an honorable surrender, their leader Kient-pos, Captain Jack, was hanged. An entrepreneur claimed his body and had it mummified. It went on tour of the East with an admission of ten cents.

Over the lip of Oklahoma Territory the Kaigwu, Kiowa, Nation rode in answer to the call of their allies, the Tsitsistas. On their left were their most hated enemies, the Texans. The soldier society of the Ka-itsen-ko, Real Dogs, kept watch in a separate line between the people and the border. It would take four more days to reach other friends, the Inde.

The Inde called the white men Pinda Lick-o-yi. White eyes. The white men called the Inde Apache. The Grant Company of Arizona paid two hundred fifty dollars for an Inde scalp. With Cochise just buried, the three bands of the Inde were led by Victorio, a Mimbreno, and Goy-ya-thle, He Who Yawns, a Chiricahua. The white men called He Who Yawns Geronimo. They also said that the two leaders would never come together, and then they had forced them together. The Ninth Cavalry was ordered to force Victorio onto the San Carlos reservation, the worst reservation in the country, where the Inde were to hoe desert under rifle guard wearing numbered discs attached to their clothes. Then the army joined the Mexicans in chasing He Who Yawns. He wasn't caught, but his wife and mother and children were murdered and mutilated for the bounty scalps and ears brought. By the time the Kaigwu would arrive, Victorio and He Who Yawns would be traveling with an extra thousand horses freshly stolen from the Ninth Cavalry.

In a force as natural and inevitable as a whirlwind, the Lakota, Tsitsistas, Kaigwu, Inde, Numa, Paiute, No-ichi, Inuna-Ina, Modoc, Banakwut, Nimipu, and Siksika swirled onto the grasslands, seventy-five thousand strong. Coming to the eye of this force was the first convoy of arms from the Canadien Service.

"Why not? It's only happened a hundred times before," General Grierson said. The hair that reached to his shoulders was black with shocks of white and his beard had the same startling contrast. Although he was fifty, Benjamin Henry Grierson was known as the Second Custer of the West.

His blue tunic was stained and dusty. The cigar he smoked left the puffing trail of a locomotive. Grierson turned his back on the aide and paced back up the hall.

"You folks have a short memory," he said. "As if the reds had never gotten together before. Never heard of Metacomet or Pontiac or Tecumseh or Blackhawk or Osceola or, hell, you people are ignorant."

"But lately . . ." the aide said. Grierson seemed as wild as an Indian to him. Being in command of the New Mexico District could do that.

"Yeah, lately," Grierson said in exasperation. "And take notes of what I'm saying, for God's sake. General Sherman can read them later at his leisure."

The aide fumbled through his desk for paper. When he was ready, Grierson went on.

"This alliance is just the latest in a series of alliances. Take the Sioux and the Cheyenne, an old alliance. Thirty years ago they became friends of the Kiowa, the Apache, and the Comanche. The Comanche happen to be very close to the Shoshone and the Paiute. The Sioux are friendly with the Blackfeet. Now, three years ago the Cheyenne made friends of the Pawnee, one of their worst enemies. The Bannock are friends with the Paiute and close to the Nez Percé, who are very tight with the Crow."

The aide stopped scribbling and looked up anxiously. Grierson walked over to the window and looked out. Outside, women with parasols were followed by children in short pants and black maids. On the St. Louis street of bricks and earth, the temperature bounced back at over one hundred.

"Well, the importance of this," Grierson said, "is that it's new, goddamn it. Sioux and Pawnee and Kiowa don't mosey up in the same tipi for no reason at all. Indians on the Plains are fighters; it's part of their life, part of their religion. They live to fight each other. When they stop fighting each other that means they're going to fight someone else, and so far as I know, we're the only opponent around. Now. . . ."

Grierson stopped as the door opened. General Sherman, commander of the armies, stood at it, a balding, paunchy man with a face glossed by sweat.

"Colonel, there must be a window in this building that is not open. Find it. Ben, come on in."

He ushered Grierson into his office, a long room that contained the heat with mahogany. Files shedding papers covered most of the floor. General Sherman brushed more papers off a chair and invited his guest to sit down.

"You'll have to excuse the colonel. Things are confused here, as you can see. Right now we're tearing the place apart to find out which of our agents is pushing the booze and the rifles. Goddamn profiteers are getting too many men killed. Sell to the army, sell to the redskins, what do they care. Every bastard west of the Missouri looks to the army as his legitimate field of profit and support."

Grierson said nothing. He rubbed his face with his hands, trying not to look at the mess on the floor. Sherman, a pale man, seemed lost in it.

"I know, I know, Ben. If I were in Washington, things would be different. It's impossible to run an army a thousand miles from Congress or your quartermaster. Orders go back and forth, assignments, countermands. The telegraph people are doing very well."

"General. Why not go back to Washington? There's a war on. We need the commander of the army in Washington. This is . . ." he gestured with his hand at the files and let it drop.

Sherman popped out of his seat, beads of sweat ringing his eyes. "Don't say that. There is no war. There are hostilities. Hostilities, that's all." He stumped to the window and fanned some air on himself, breathing slowly to calm down. "As for me being in Washington, as soon as the president decides whose advice he will take on military affairs, mine or the War Department's, I'll go back. Until then, as a matter of honor, not only mine but the United States Army's, I shall remain here in St. Louis. At any rate, an election is approaching and we will be seeing the last of Ulysses. Then we can return in triumph, not in disgrace. In the meantime, General, why don't you get along with your report."

"Yes, General," Grierson said. He had tried and failed. He never thought that he could convince Sherman to abandon his exile in this province town of tanners and brewers. "The situation. The uprising is general. The Ninth Cavalry has fifty percent casualties. Santa Fe and Fort Apache are the only places I can guarantee safety. Last I heard as I left was that the Pueblo and Navaho were putting down their blankets, which is . . ."

"Ridiculous." Sherman stabbed a black cheroot at him. "Apache but not Pueblo."

"Oh, no? Thirty years ago was the last time they got off their asses. They took over the state and scalped the governor. Thirteen years ago it was the Sioux, the Arapaho, and the Cheyenne after the governor of Colorado announces he wants them killed. Announces, if you can believe it! The next thing you know is Denver is under siege. You don't tell the Indians these things; they're not dumb animals. You kill them but you don't tell them in advance. Every tribe has been active, every tribe has been getting smarter, every tribe has been sending out feelers to the others. I'm only giving you the outline of something that must be as plain as, Christ, the nose on the president's face. So why do you say it's ridiculous?"

Sherman smiled grimly and took a telegraph from the inside of his tunic. "This is why, General. It's a message I received today, telling me that Congress has set a new limit on the size of the Army of the United States. You remember that we demanded an increase from thirty thousand to fifty thousand. We got twenty-five thousand."

"You mean, twenty-five thousand more."

"No, General. Twenty-five thousand. Period. So, when you tell me that we have a war in the Department of the West, the Department of New Mexico, the Department of Arizona, and the Department of Utah, I know and you know that it's ridiculous."

Both men were quiet. Grierson realized for the first time the strain the General was working under, cut off from a friend who had become president and betrayed him to a Congress that treated the army as a company of lepers and thieves. He was a hero; they were all heroes who had been pushed aside by a country that was busy making money. And now that the country had stopped making money and was in the middle of the Great Depression, they had simply been ignored. All the old heroes had left were cigars and whiskey.

Sherman pulled out a desk drawer as if he were telepathic and raised a bottle. A pair of shot glasses appeared and the general poured out two stiff doses.

"Hell, Ben, have some leopard sweat and relax a bit. We can't get screaming at each other."

Grierson took his and knocked it down. Sherman poured a second round. "There've been Indian scares before and there'll be Indian scares again. We'll get through. It'll mean arming some militia, using some more scouts, I know. We'll do it. Then we'll go back to Congress for some new appropriations. Life goes on. That make you feel better?"

Grierson gritted his teeth and smiled. He let his weary body fold up in the chair. A real bed with a goose down throw was what he wanted, something out of childhood.

Sherman tapped the bottle. "George Custer was getting funny last time I saw him. Took his whiskey with sugar, Indian style. I heard that's the way he liked his women, too. That's why his wife . . . oh, let the dead rest. Think he let himself walk into something?"

Grierson found a filing box he could rest his feet on.

"No more than the rest of us. Who expected half the Sioux Nation? You really want to know what I think?"

Sherman sat on his desk, his bone-dry eyes fixing on Grierson. "I didn't ask you to ride for a week to come here and lie. Just don't go off exaggerating. Newspapers get hold of that sort of thing and they'll make it into another massacre. Go on."

"It's difficult. There's nothing definite, but I've been in command of the Department of New Mexico for seven years now and I can sense things. Things have changed. Times have changed."

"Of course," Sherman said. "More and more settlers, homesteaders, lunatics looking for gold. I see them going through St. Louis every day, wagon trains of them. And railroads, they've changed the West. And the buffalo, there's less of them. I say the trains are going to kill the Indians off, Phil Sheridan says it'll be the buffalo. Either way, in enough time there won't be any problem. Just a few rotgut drunks to push off a cliff."

"No. That's how things were. Things have changed. We've been taking the territory a little at a time, a thousand little bites. We've been winning a continent with a two-bit war of attrition against a world of naive primitives too ignorant and confused to stop digging their own graves. That's what I think has changed. I think there's real organization this time. There's more Indians than people think. Do you know how many Indians fought in the War? Ten thousand. I'm not saying that veterans are mixed up in this thing, but I am saying that the nibbling has stopped. The real fighting has begun."

Sherman shook his head. The Indian Wars were the creation of the dime novels. It was moments like this that he envied Sheridan going off to watch firsthand the Prussians slaughter the French. That would have been a war to watch.

"You promised you wouldn't exaggerate, Ben. I'm ordering you to get some sleep. You're all in, beat. As for the Indians, forget about them. The president is merely reaping the harvest of his new policy. I told him long ago that unless the redman was exterminated that he would live forever as a pauper at our national expense. Well, when the Indians head for their winter camps we'll track them down and burn them, every mother's son we find. And the more Indians we kill this year, the fewer we have to kill next year. That's what I call a policy."

Grierson could tell the interview was over and he didn't care. Sherman was slapping him on the back like a hearty Lilliputian. He didn't believe him. Who remembered the Cheyenne charging at the call of a bugle at Adobe Walls in '74? Sherman, who had been faced down by the Dog Soldiers ten years before, was back

East and had forgotten. All those people east of some supernatural line drawn north from San Antonio were from another world. Grierson imagined them on a stage, building their factories and cooking their pies and going to school, unaware that in the rear of the theater there was a struggle going on with real blood and bullets, and a horde of real savages ready to descend on them. It would never happen, not to people in St. Louis or Washington or Philadelphia. That's why they lived in another world.

"You stick with me on this, Ben, and I think I can promise you another star."

Grierson found himself out of the office and the foyer and into the street. The boards of the sidewalk measured his progress to a civilized hotel.

>►◄◄

Passenger Dionicio Duran arrived in Washington from Mexico City in the early morning. He was a short, swarthy man with a pencil mustache accenting his wiry build. An ornately tooled attaché case complemented the sharp cut of his suit. His neighbor on the flight welcomed Dulles's grey stripes with a sigh after an endless tirade on tariffs offered by Sr. Duran.

"I am very proud of my English because I practice it," Duran said with his hands out.

"Yes, yes, you do," the importer from Roanoke admitted. He turned down an invitation to a drink in the airport bar by inventing a wife in the parking lot.

"*Hasta luego*," Duran said without offense. He took his attaché case and raincoat and ambled to customs, whistling.

There were no hitches with the passport. Duran picked up a taxi and let himself be swept away onto the grass-bordered highway that ran into the city. Washington was not new to him.

He checked into a room on the second floor at the Mayflower, a single with a bath, a television, and a Bible. As soon as he locked the door he threw his jacket and shirt off and washed his face with cold water. The bed's mattress was soft and uncomfortable, but he was determined to sleep.

It was dark, early evening when he was awake again. Still, he could make out the features of the room with no trouble. The print of the Pilgrims stepping onto a beach, holding their crosses high to exorcise any possible demons. The telephone. Wallpaper in a mountain laurel pattern. A cardboard triangle on the desk with a picture of a family boarding a recommended tour. The metal bureau with the Realwood finish.

Duran rolled off the bed and flicked the television on. The picture rolled and rolled. He left it as it was and went back to the bathroom. As he shaved off his mustache, he could hear the set. It seemed to be a variety show and a comedian was in the middle of his monologue.

". . . Sure, we all have problems. I make a good living, got two beautiful kids, lovely wife, two cars. But I pay for it. I got a mother-in-law. I pay. Now, take the Cheyenne. A Cheyenne husband isn't allowed to speak to his mother-in-law and she's not allowed to speak to him. That's the law. And we call them stupid. Hah! Someday I'm going to come home with a war bonnet on and the first word she says—*pow!* In the head with the tomahawk. You like it?"

Duran lost ten years with the mustache. The spot above his lip looked a little more olive than the rest of his skin, but not much. He trimmed his sideburns, thoroughly pleased at being able to recognize himself.

". . . of course. Being a Cheyenne is not all peaches and buffalo stew. I mean, a Cheyenne guy wants a break from the Big Chief In The Sky, he has to promise to do something. You know what he promises? Not sleep with his wife for a while. For a while? Seven years. He gets a promotion at work and he doesn't sleep with his wife for seven years. Actually, it's not the sleeping that I'd miss, I'll tell you that right now. It's the stuff you do when you're not sleeping. If I were a Cheyenne, I'd try to work out some sort of compromise."

He took his pants off and hung them up with the suit jacket in the closet. There was another conservative suit in the attaché case that he put on with a new tie. In the inside pocket of the fresh suit was a United States passport with a new name. He took the embossed plastic cover off the attaché and cut it into shreds so that it would flush down the toilet. When he was finished, he did the same with the Mexican passport.

". . . Folks, you've been a great audience. So I'd like to leave you with a valuable piece of advice. As General Custer once said, 'Don't take any wooden Indians.' Thank you, thank you."

The last thing Duran did before he left the room was check a velvet box inside the undecorated attaché case. He opened the box as if it contained an icon. Cushioned in red velvet forms were a pair of self-cocking, double-action Irish Constabulary pistols with pearl handles.

When he left the room, the television rolled on, its voice unattached to a head.

Chapter Two

Father, paint the earth on me,
A nation I will make over!

—Sun Dance

There was nothing to compare the Plains to. The grass savannahs stretched for a thousand miles in every direction. A man could ride for a month without finding an end to its dimension. Blue grama, big blue grass, buffalo grass, and three-awns, wild grass with roots six feet deep covered the land. Where the soil was bad, bottle brush, fool hay, jungle rice, red ray, pancake, and panic grass survived. From a thousand feet up, the millions of buffalo roaming this greatest grassland in the world would have seemed more like schools of small, brown fish feeding from a limitless ocean.

In September, two months after the death of Custer, General Crook, whom the Indians knew as Nan-tan Lupan or Grey Wolf, began his invasion. Into the grass came troops from Fort Fetterman, Fort A. Lincoln, and Fort Ellis. The long caravan rode behind its vanguard of scouts, searching for the dispersed camps.

The first trail struck was that of American Horse, a Lakota. It was the largest trail they had ever seen, the grass almost trampled from unshod horses.

General MacKenzie was ordered to follow it. He was given eleven companies of cavalry from the Second, Third, and Fifth Regiments, four companies from the Fourth Artillery, dismounted, and eleven infantry companies from the Fourth, Ninth, Fourteenth and Twenty-Fifth Regiments. Crook was to follow and take command of the battle, with MacKenzie leading the horse brigades and Colonel Dodge in charge of the foot soldiers.

In front of the soldiers were the scouts, four hundred of them—Pawnee, renegade Lakota, Inuna-ina, Shoshone, Banakwut, and Tsitsistas. Major North, a squaw man, led the two hundred Pawnee as usual, William Rowland led the few Tsitsistas, and the Shoshone followed Chief Washakie. The rest were commanded by Captain Amos Mills. Behind scouts and soldiers was a support force of wagons, seven ambulances, and four hundred mules. The packers and mulewhackers totaled another two hundred eighty-five men. General Crook was a firm believer in logistics after the Battle of the Rosebud.

At the same time, another line of logistics was in operation from another direction, from Grandmother's Land, Canada.

The Canadien Service had been operating for two hundred years, a race of mixed French-Indian-Negro bloods traveling from Mexico to Canada with the trade and contraband of every season. The Americans called them animals. One of the bloods could carry six ninety-pound packs for a portage of five miles. This time, down the Missouri, the Milk, and the Little Milk Rivers in boats, and across land on foot and wagons, they carried ammunition, dried meat, and cloth bolts.

The meat was from Australia, where the Great Depression

left millions of unshorn, unprofitable sheep. The rifles and bullets had come by route of Connecticut to England to Turkey to Canada. They were the products of a New Haven shirt manufacturer named Oliver F. Winchester and were center-fire cartridge repeaters called Model 73's, rejected by the United States government as not sufficiently tested.

Other governments approved of them, though, and Winchester had a close relationship with the British, who acted as middleman for large Near East and Far East sales. Winchester's top agent was "Colonel" Tom Addis, who by himself had delivered and taken the payment for one thousand repeaters from Benito Juarez's Mexican soldiers. It was a small sale compared to those Winchester and Addis made to colonial armies in China and India and for the seventy thousand rifles ordered by the Turks in London. There is little reason to believe that Winchester was aware of the real destination of the arms marked for the Ottomans; there is no reason to believe that Addis was not fully aware, as the later government investigation found, but he was a man driven by a compulsion to sell a product.

Crates marked with vouchers of the sale went from New Haven to England and on to the Mediterranean. The rifles, however, went from New Haven to Newfoundland. One out of four Indians at the Greasy Grass was armed with them. The Canadien Service was bringing the bulk of the order, repeaters with a range of only two hundred yards compared to the six hundred yards of the single-shot Springfields, but with an action that would not jam; short, light, the best on-horse weapon ever invented.

The mules carried equipage that had been thoroughly tested by the United States: surplus Civil War mountain howitzers sold by the quartermaster's office. The cannons could shoot canister or shell ammunition. Against troops the canister was used, with its one hundred forty-eight musket balls arranged in four tiers. A whole howitzer with carriage, ammunition, tools, and portable forge weighed three quarters of a ton and needed two mules to haul it. On other mules were Gorloff guns, a five-barrelled gun that fired one thousand rounds in a short burst, a Russian copy of the Gatling.

In barges and on trails they headed for Crazy Woman Fork in the Powder River Valley, Yellow Nose's camp of Tsitsistas. Here the chiefs of the many nations were gathering, warriors from the different corners of the Great Plains who had heard of but never seen each other, the last great chiefs all arriving with a train of glory, finery, anxiety, and high anticipation.

The pipe went from left to right. It was the custom of the Tsitsistas, the Cheyenne, that no man could lie after smoking it. At least, no Indian could lie. Yellow Nose, as it was his camp— with the women drying buffalo hides under the sun, the girls playing with corn husk dolls, and the boys choosing sides for killing-all-the-soldiers—had the honor of going first, puffing the sacred number of four puffs to the four directions. In battle he would have a yellow stripe across his face. Now he wore only a modest notched eagle feather for one enemy's slit throat.

Two Moons, the young Tsitsistas war chief, smoked next, a fat-faced man who commanded his own camp. On his left was They Fear His Horses, slender, his face as sharp as an arrow-head's, his hair falling in two plain braids, who gave away all he owned so that his power would not be damaged by envy, who was watched by every other man in the great tipi of thirty painted skins. Gall was next, then White Bull, then He Who Yawns, the Inde, shorter and darker than the others, wearing a buckskin cap painted with patterns of the seasons and a shirt splendid with bright beads.

He handed the pipe on to Victorio, who wore a yellow vest of racing antelope and squatted on boots tied at the knee. Big

Lake, the Siksika, taller by a head, was in white shirt and leggings edged with ermine tails. A circle of eagle feathers set in an ermine base crowned his head. The arrogant Kaigwu, Black Horse, muscular but tending to fat, perhaps the finest horseman of all, smoked and passed the pipe on. Arrow and Ignacio, stocky men in clothes that were part farmer's and part warrior's, smoked for the Ute Nation. The Banakwut chief, Buffalo Horn, his eyes dancing with fervor, smoked with long fingers that shook.

Other chiefs took their turns. Iron Shirt, who went into battle with a cuirass left by the Conquistadors; Calf; Quanah Parker; grey-haired Jumper in a formal black suit; the fighting chief of all the Tsitsistas, Brave Wolf; Sleeping Rabbit; Hawks Visit; Bull Hump; Burns Red; Coal Bear; White Thunder; the spiritual Black Hairy Dog who kept the sacred arrows; Crow King; and the vicious Black Moon all puffed in turn the blessed tobacco.

As the pipe came round full circle it rested in the hands of Wovoka, the young visionary with the blocky face and close-cropped hair. Then to a slight man, fair with brown hair that hung over one ear who dressed in a loin cloth and a long, fringed buckskin shirt, the one called John Setter by the whites and Where The Sun Goes by the chiefs. At last, the pipe rested in the hands of Sitting Bull, the long-nosed, dour *wichasha wakon*, holy man, of the Lakota. He pressed his thin lips in silence.

All watched him. Not only the men who had smoked but the warrior and messengers from all the other tribes who sat with their backs against the gloom of the tipi walls. A Dine in clothes of grass and rabbit fur, with his hair in a black knot; an Absasoke with his hair in a statuesque pompadour and wearing a bib of quills; an Omaha with feathered braids that reached to his waist; Ollicut, who was brother to Thunder Going Over The Mountain; a squat Modoc next to him; a Shoshoni with tattooed arms; a Pima from the south; an Okanagan with his bear coat open on his chest; Stand Watie of the Cherokee; a Lenape with a high collar; a Choctaw and an Alabama, each in wide-brimmed hats; members from all six nations of the League of the Ongwanosionni. Standing at the entrance were two Dog Soldiers, one of the Lakota and one of the Tsitsistas.

"The soldiers are buried on the Greasy Grass," Sitting Bull said at last. "That is why we are here now. Soon there will be more soldiers. Will we be here then? Will we be here after?

"If we do not resist, if we go back to the agencies as we are ordered to do, to let some of us be hung in the coward's death and the rest to scratch at the earth where the Wasichu tell us to, let us do so now. Let us talk no further, let us say nothing. We shall go home like squaws, in silence, and let them do with us as they will. Myself, I have no stomach for arguing, for making more treaties, for hesitating a heart's beat longer. But if you do, then let us leave now for there is no point in staying longer in this spot. As for myself, The World Maker made me an Indian—but not an agency Indian."

There was another long silence as each man looked at the medicine bags in the center of the tipi so that any leaving would not be embarrassed by notice. When Sitting Bull spoke again the same number were listening.

"A long time ago, there was another wichasha wakon among the Lakota who was called Wooden Cup. This great man had immense powers and was well loved, but he died a sad man. He saw a vision of the future of the Lakota in which a strange people came from the direction of the sunrise. He said that there would be more of them than the numbers of the buffalo. And then the buffalo would turn to bones all across the prairies. Our Mother Earth would be bound with hoops of iron. Our sacred ring, the circle of the Lakota, he said, would be smashed by the magic of the strangers and finally, in the end, his people would live in little square grey houses and in those houses they would starve. That is what he saw.

"That is what has been happening to the Lakota. I, who have seen fifty summer hunts, know it is so. I can remember when Father Washington begged for our favors so that he might send people, strangers, across the land; when soldiers came in peace and looked around at the endless grass and sky, they said it was so big that there was room for all. And then they asked for just a little bit. And then just a little bit more. And more, and more, and more. Our friend Where The Sun Goes tells me of a chief called Metacomet, long dead, who told a story that when the first Wasichu came to this land he asked the Indians for only as much land as he could cover with his blanket. They said that was good, and then he unraveled his blanket into one long string that stretched forever and covered the horizon. I do not want to be covered.

"The old chief of the Lakota, Red Cloud, who was a great warrior, is not with us. He has fought and surrendered and gone to the places New York and Washington and come back and told us not to fight anymore. He is brave and wise and he tells us that we must not continue in the old ways, that we must become as much Wasichu as we can if we want to survive. However, a Lakota does not believe that it is good to die an old man without glory, so we will fight. It may be foolish, for both Wooden Cup and Red Cloud had great powers, but we will do so, dying as Lakota rather than living like dogs between the kicks of Wasichu."

He paused and fondled the medicine bag in front of him, a parfleche with the bones of the bull he had killed as a young man to fulfill his vision.

"Now I am told, as you have been told, that we can choose more than a good death. For the vision of Wooden Cup, we have the vision of Tavibo and his son Wovoka. For the knowledge Red

Cloud has of the Wasichu, we have the knowledge of Where The Sun Goes. They are good men and I believe what they say is true. You think so also or you would not be here."

He Who Yawns grunted with impatience. Setter smiled without changing his face. The Inde was an orator who loved to use his talents. Setter remembered when they first met over the Mexican border in the mountains and the bow-legged chief strutted and spoke for an entire day with just one man and a snow-thawed stream for an audience.

"The guns. Let us talk about the guns," He Who Yawns said.

"We will," Sitting Bull said. "But first we must talk of the vision. Guns without a vision are nothing. We will listen to Wovoka now."

It was not unusual for a seer of visions to be young. The Spirit revealed himself early in a man's life so that he might take his name, and some came so close to God that they were not like other men again. In Wovoka's broad, open face the eyes flickered like coals. He spoke slowly since it was the Paiute custom for a listener to repeat everything he had heard so that the speaker might correct any errors. No one repeated now since they were not Paiute, but after each sentence he looked about to see if there were any questions on the faces that surrounded him.

"The Wanekiah, the Messiah, is coming to the Indian. He has been spurned by the Wasichu and he has chosen us. All will be resurrected by Him. All except the Wasichu will rise. All dead Indians, all the dead buffalo, the old ways of living. We must dance around a circle with no fire. We must sing new songs. Then, when all are reborn, the Indians will have this land again and we will take what we want from what is left of the Wasichu world. This is the vision of my father. This is my vision."

After a period of respectable contemplation, Black Horse asked, "Why does the Wanekiah turn from his own people?"

"Because they have turned from him. They are too clever so that they live like rats that mindlessly steal all they can from everyone else without knowing what they have. So that they have power, but they no longer have the power that He gave them. He is giving us that power."

"How did you achieve this vision?" Ignacio asked. He knew but, like all of them, he wanted to hear again.

"In the high desert, I fasted until I was dead. It was then that Wanekiah came to me and spoke and then He brought me back to life. The winter after, I met Where The Sun Goes."

Outside, the men passed the time gambling with sticks, singing their private songs to chance, and making their throws on the ground pounded hard by ponies. Inside, the chiefs asked more questions of the seer, giving his answers by heart to the background of muffled chants and laughs. When they were satisfied, even the sophisticated Savane, as the nations from the East were called, they turned to Setter.

"I am from the Metutahanke, the Mandan, the father of the tribes of the Plains," Setter said to the acknowledging grunts of the tipi. He spread his hands wide as he spoke, encompassing them. Silver streaked his brown hair. "You know me and my people. We were once very powerful as you are now powerful, and the Wasichu from many nations feared us. The United States sent us gifts, England sent us pleas to be their friends, and the French sent us men in black, the Jesuits. Then only Father Washington was left and yet he did not dare to fight us. He asked for our trust. So we trusted him and he sent more gifts, blankets—though we didn't need them, for our camps were rich from trading the length of the Missouri; our long lodges facing the rising sun had thousands of hides for the winter.

"We did not know that we were envied, that Wasichu traders wanted the river for themselves, and that Father Washington did also. So we took the thin, musty blankets and soon we began dying. The blankets had been tainted with *wicranran*, smallpox, by the traders. In a few moments, there were not many Metutahanke left on the banks of the Missouri. Out of three thousand, only thirty remained. Most of the survivors were scarred. I was a boy then, and for some reason I lived and had no pocks.

"One of the men in black took me north and educated me and I became valuable to him. I was able to travel not only to Washington but across the sea to Grandmother England and other places. Red Cloud says that the Wasichu are more numerous than the buffalo, and he is right. But when he says that we cannot defeat them, he is wrong. We are many. Consider this. Of the nations within the grasslands, we are four times greater than their army. Of the nations that will join us, that must join us for their own sake because that is the only way any Indian will live, we are ten times greater than their army.

"What is their power? Let me tell you. An elephant is a creature that lives in a far land. It is big, ten times the size of a big buffalo, and it has weak eyes, ugly skin, and a long nose for grabbing things. The power of the Wasichu is as the carcass of a rotting elephant, itself dying with sickness but grabbing everything it finds as it rolls along to its death.

"We should fear them? Who fights for them against us? Indians. Look at the troops of Grey Fox and Miles. Half Indian. Without the Shoshone, Grey Fox would have been dead at the Rosebud. If the Shoshone joined their brothers, if the Pawnee and Lenape and Crow joined their brothers, the Wasichu would not be able to find their way back to their wooden towns. If men like Jumper and Stand Watie, who were colonels and majors during the war between the states and are spit on now by Wasichu drunks, joined their brothers with their nations, no Wasichu troops would ever slaughter another Indian camp.

"The vision of Wovoka is true. We can see the Indian reborn, but not by dying. By winning." Setter cast a look at He Who Yawns, who was squirming with silent questions. "Guns? We shall have repeaters better than the soldiers. We will have big guns, too, and see how the Wasichu like their own medicine. And food, though we should not hesitate to kill any Wasichu killing buffalo. But none of this is enough without the vision. The vision you must keep before your eyes always."

He rubbed his hand over his face, which had turned strangely old while he spoke, almost betraying him at the moment he had worked so long for. In the gloom of the tipi, the twisting fumes of the pipe suddenly seemed like the shadow of a rose window, the colors of the young scholar in his sacristy. Setter nudged Wovoka, who carried on.

"To bring back the old way," Wovoka said, "we must not become like the Wasichu, but we must not make the old mistakes. This the Wanekiah told me we must do.

"Trust no Wasichu. No matter how good a friend, he will betray you before he betrays his own kind.

"Count no more coups. War is a struggle for our lives, not a competition for honors. Be like They Fear His Horses, who has never stopped to feed his coup lance. The Wasichu knows no honor and stabs the vain warrior in the back as he takes a scalp.

"The Indian who murders another Indian stinks in the nostrils of the Wanekiah. From now on, the Lakota is the friend of the Chippewa, the Modoc is the brother of the Choctaw. It is a Tsitsistas custom that the killer is putrid, and the Wanekiah says it is so for all the peoples."

"*Siquism*," He Who Yawns said. "The word for brother among the Inde is siquism."

By the time the council was over, it was night and a thousand fires lined Crazy Woman. Few of the men spoke as they left for their own lodges. Setter staggered with fatigue but Victorio and He Who Yawns each had one of his arms and were dragging him to their fire. Victorio was convivial, but the Chiricahua was spilling over with dammed-up words. Compared to the elegance of some of the lodges, the Inde was poor, just a windbreak for the generals of seven thousand fighters.

"I know what it was like for you when you lost your family," he said. "It was the same with me. To see their bodies! I did not pray nor did I decide to do anything for I had no purpose left. I could have gone into Mexico with my men, we could have saved those of the tribe who had been taken for slaves. But I did nothing for a long time." He Who Yawns sighed and slumped down on his side on a blanket. He tossed a strip of meat sweet with chili to Setter. "Not much but it will fill your stomach, I promise. No, I did nothing."

Victorio rolled cornmeal and honey into a ball and popped it into his mouth. He smiled. "Dodge The Apache Killer, he calls my friend the worst Indian who ever lived. I think he must have done something sometime."

A twisted grin spread over He Who Yawns. "Agents cheat the Inde all the time and all they say are bad things about He Who Yawns. Someday, if you like, I will ride into Tucson and find the men who moved the Inde reservation to San Carlos so that we would not be able to grow anything and have to buy from them. I will find them and tie them upside down over a little fire and we will eat their boiled brains when it rolls out of the eyes."

Setter looked at the cornmeal ball Victorio had given him and flipped it over his shoulder.

After a while, the man known to the newspapers as "The Human Tiger" began yawning and Setter was able to move on to another campfire. It was a large one with pots of coffee brewing over the coals. Stand Watie was rolling a cigarette with a piece of newspaper. Men from the nations of the Savane, Choctaw, Seneca, Seminole, and others sat in their broadcloth suits and watched Setter intently.

"We were just talking about you," Jumper said. The fire lit up the fleshy curves of the Seminole's face. "Just talking when speak of the devil. You've really got some steam up here, Mr. Setter. Big ideas. We're still wondering, though."

Jumper, natty in his storeclothes, seemed to be speaking for all of them. Setter sat down as casually as he could. "You've got some questions? Shoot."

"This is the question," Stand Watie said. He took the rest of the newspaper and dropped it at Setter's feet. "Pick it up. Read it."

Setter glanced at it and saw the banner head, *The Phoenix*. "I know the paper," he said. "It's the paper of the Cherokee and a good one."

"That's right," Jumper said. "Cherokee paper for educated Cherokee, people who have their own government recognized by Congress. Just as the educated Choctaw have their own government which is recognized by Congress. So what makes you think that we, any of the civilized tribes, would throw in with a bunch of savages?"

"The Ongwanosionni, the League of the Long House, agrees. The Seneca and Mohawk and the rest aren't about to rebel against the government. We fought for the Union, not so we could secede," a man without an arm said.

"The Lenni Lenape have always had a special relationship with the United States," another said. "They need us for scouts and we have always fought well for them. Besides, we are Christian now. Primitive chants don't impress us, only rifles."

The ring of eyes in seamed dark skin and funeral suits weighed on Setter. He sensed that pleading would only increase their arrogance. The Easterners had been dumped like cattle in

Oklahoma and they thought they were back ruling their Atlantic forests.

"So," Setter said, "you want to know what you have in common with other men with red skin, these savages that are hooting around you, thinking they can defy the United States Army. I mean, you have your own governments recognized by Congress. Very impressive. Good.

"Just like Congress recognized the Cherokee Nation back in Georgia. You turned Christian. Sequoyah made you an alphabet and you were the richest, most powerful farmers in the state. So what happened to you, to your recognition by Congress. Some land developers got the state to take your farms away and the army rounded you up and marched you to Oklahoma.

"One of every three Cherokee died on the way and the Indian Commissioner said it was a 'striking example of liberality,' that 'the hazard of an effusion of blood has been put by and we have quietly and gently transported eighteen thousand friends to the west bank of the Mississippi.' That's what your recognition from Congress got you."

"That was forty years ago," Stand Watie said.

"Sure, and when they find something else they want from you they'll take it. Maybe they'll want your new land because even though it's miserable, someone will invent a use for it, or they'll want your water, or send you to die in wars for themselves like they did in the Rebellion or to kill other Indians. You make fools of yourselves with your games of self-government and you know it. Don't look down on other Indians who don't want to be fools."

A Lenape walked behind Setter and took out his handgun, a .50 caliber Springfield, and cocked it behind Setter's head. He began speaking in a low, grim voice.

"Look, you leech-sucking breed, I didn't come all the way

from Kansas to have you call me a fool. Now, you apologize or, by God, I'll blow your goddamn head off."

Setter turned to look into the heavy gun. "It depends. What nation are you from?"

"Delaware, Lenape, whatever you want to call it. I want to hear an apology from you and you've got ten seconds to make it."

The men of the Savane sat in silence. None of them would help. Setter looked around. The nearest camps were Piegan Siksika, forty feet away. Too far. "Lenape, huh? Famous treaty with William Penn giving them their land to perpetuity. Sold out to gain favor with the Seneca, your enemies. Dumped in Kansas, later in Oklahoma. Sold out and shipped off right down the line by the same folks you want to kill me for. And for what? For saying that your Wasichu pals have been stabbing you in the back. For saying the truth. If that's what you want to kill me for, then go right ahead."

The Lenape looked down over the sight, a mercenary, the way most of the Lenape were for the past hundred years. After ten seconds, his thumb came down on the hammer and eased it home, safely. Setter immediately ignored him and turned back to the others.

"And remember this, all you proud men. When the blood starts flowing, you're going to be in it whether you want to be or not. The Wasichu doesn't know the difference between a bad Indian and a good Indian. A month after we start out, a pack of drunk vigilantes are going to come riding through your happy reservations, shooting your children and raping your wives. Then you'll know what side you're on but then it will be too late. Choose your sides now, not then.

"And remember this, too. When the war is over and the Indians control this vast land, the opportunities for the educated ones will be very great. Good night, gentlemen."

Setter stood up and walked slowly toward the Siksika fire. Cold beads of sweat sat on his lips. He felt drained of his last reserves of energy and his moccasins seemed to sink into the ground. A cool breeze blew off the river. No bullets came tearing through his back from the Savane. Big Lake came out to meet him.

"How!"

"How now!"

"Cola!"

"It is an honor for you to come to our camp. I promise you that no speeches are necessary. We have made up our minds. That burden is behind us so we can relax."

The tall chief led Setter to a buffalo hide couch. His wife served a stew of jerky and corn in a leather bowl. A Lakota and a Siksika were playing the guessing game, one watching as the other switched a rabbit's foot from hand to hand faster than the eye could watch. The bet was a pair of racing ponies. Also watching and joking was They Fear His Horses.

"They are champions," Big Lake said. "The Lakota is one of special society that follows They Fear His Horses, the Ho-ksi-ha-ka-ta, the Last-Born Sons. Here."

Big Lake offered Setter a treat, a buffalo liver pulled from the fire and smeared with marrow. Setter ate it and grunted with appreciation.

"You are getting like an elephant," They Fear His Horses told the Lakota gambler, "whatever an elephant is. All I know is that it's big and slow, like a Wasichu horse."

"Eat up," Big Lake said. "Tomorrow the Lakota begin the Sun Dance and people will be fasting."

Gall, the Lakota, sat down by Setter. He was a muscular, big-jawed man. He reminded Setter of Ajax, trustworthy but not terribly intelligent. When they were talking about treaties, Sitting Bull told Setter that Gall would sign anything for a square meal.

"They will be with us, don't you think?" he asked Setter.

"Sooner or later."

Big Lake leaned close to Setter. "In Grandmother's Country, they are letting the nations roam where they will, especially if they roam south on the plains. It was when I saw this happening that I knew you were telling the truth."

Gall grabbed a piece of liver for himself and swabbed marrow on it like a slab of butter and gulped down the steaming mass in one bite. "Delicious," he said. "It reminds me of the Indian agent Myrich at Fort Ridgely. One winter we were starving and he was selling the meat that was sent for us. We demanded the food and he said, 'Let them eat grass.' So we killed him and stuffed his mouth with grass. That was, oh, ten, fifteen years ago. A good joke. We killed eight hundred soldiers that time."

Big Lake looked into the fire and the embers that spun into the air. He was lean, aristocratic in his ivory buckskin. "They have no visions, the Wasichu," he said. "That was a hard thing for me to believe at first. How could you know what your name would be without a vision? It's no wonder they want so much with no vision to guide them. That, I think, is the big difference between them and us, not color."

The Lakota opened his hand to reveal the rabbit foot amid howls of triumph from the watchers. Setter made his excuses and wandered away from the ring around the fire. Things were going well enough; the camp fires stretched for miles. Sitting Bull and Wovoka were circulating, too, to answer questions. He could go to sleep.

A hand gripped his arm. It was They Fear His Horses. Shouts erupted in the rear where the game had started again.

"I have just a few things I wanted to ask you and I did not want to embarrass you in front of everyone," the Oglala Lakota said. "Perhaps we can talk here."

Setter nodded and they sat on the grass of the bank in the dark. There seemed to be no horizon between the stars and the endless fires.

"Anything you want to know," Setter said.

They Fear His Horses obviously had some trouble getting out what he wanted to say, waiting until he had the question phrased exactly right for a minimum of discomfort for Setter.

"The first rule of the new ways is that we are to trust no whites. Yet the arms we are receiving and the food, they are all coming from the whites. Are we trusting the other whites? What do they want for helping us that we should trust them? It just does not make any sense to me." He said the last words rapidly to get them over with but even in the blackness Setter had the sensation that he was being earnestly studied by the war leader.

"We trust no whites," Setter said. "The new ones want just what the soldiers want, everything we have."

"Then what is the difference?"

"The only difference is that they are farther away."

"What happens when they come for payment?"

"We will give them what we want to give them, not what they want to take. What will stop them from taking what they want? They and the United States are two hungry wolves after the same young elk. They will be so busy fighting each other that by the time one wins the elk will have his antlers and kill that wolf forever."

They Fear His Horses pondered the explanation. Finally, he exploded, "*Washtay!* I like it. That is a vision I like. To me you are Lakota, a friend. You have a power, you know. I can feel it."

The two of them followed the invisible trail of a nighthawk screeching through the night.

"It's called economics," Setter said.

The guns arrived the next day with the sun. For the last ten miles a wave of riders led by American Horse rode on the banks alongside the barges full of breeds and mules as they drifted down the Powder River. Lines formed to haul the barges up on land under direction of the Dog Soldier societies. The mules were led off with a great splashing of water from the weight of the cannon parts. They Fear His Horses and Brave Wolf inspected each crate of repeaters as they came on shore, their satisfaction growing with each box. Even Jumper, who had officered in the war, was impressed with the quantity of arms as the barges began filling the banks. Victorio filled a rifle and emptied its clip in ten seconds. The rifles were handed out according to war societies. Jumper found himself beside the mules, looking over the dismantled cannons.

"Familiar?" he was asked. Two Moons stood behind him, running his hand over the metal barrel. "I'm sorry. I didn't mean to startle you."

"Nothing," Jumper said. "I just keep forgetting that some of you people can speak English. My fault. Yeah, it's familiar, okay. Mountain gun. Hasn't changed a bit. I was just wondering if any of you knew how to use it, that's all."

Two Moons shook his head. "No. I don't and I don't know of anyone in my nation who does. We've never had them before."

Jumper screwed his forehead. "Well, how the hell do you intend to use it?"

"Someone who knows will come along," the Tsitsistas said blandly. "So I do not worry."

"Jesus!" Jumper said with exasperation. He took off his jacket and folded it neatly over a saddle. "Until that lucky man comes along, at least let me show you how to put one of these bastards together so you don't blow yourself up."

The arrangements for the Sun Dance were underway when the first rifle was unloaded. The *chun wakon,* the sacred tree, had been secured, a slender cottonwood. The branches had been cut off by two girls of good reputation and it was placed in a level ground enclosed by tipi skins that opened in the center to the sun. Sitting Bull painted the tree red and tied chokecherry limbs onto the tree crotch so that his fingers were stained with the holy color. When the hole for planting was ready, he dropped a piece of buffalo tallow into it as an offering to the Earth Mother, Maka, and then the tree was set into place. After the long thongs had been tied from the top of the tree, everything was ready for the dancers. The arms had been unloaded and the breeds of the Canadien Service banqueted. Everyone looked to the rising of the next sun.

Thirty dancers were in a closed lodge, preparing themselves with sweat baths while priests rubbed their backs and chests with sacred sage and painted them red all over. The principal dancers would be the men who first spotted Custer—Calf, Roan Horse, and Bobtail Horse.

They came out from the lodge between two lines of Lakota, Roan Horse first, carrying a huge buffalo skull, the men in their full war bonnets and the women with flowers braided through their hair. It was still before dawn as messengers and warriors from the other nations joined the spectators and the dancers reached the dancing ground. Roan Horse led the dancers in a slow circle around the tree, their skin painted red, shivering from the cold. The others filled the sides of the enclosure, those with brothers or sons in the dance solemn with pride.

The open circle above the tree suddenly turned from blue to silver to gold. The sun had risen. The dancers stopped where they were. Drums of taut hide and wood slat tied to skins started beating to the slap of sticks, their sound echoing off the buffalo walls and returning to the voices of the drummers. The watchers shouted with excitement. As one, the drummers and dancers stopped and Roan Horse went in a lone circle around the tree. With no hurry, he thrust the buffalo skull three times onto a mound of white clay. The fourth time he left the skull on top of it. Sitting Bull came out to him with a pipe decorated with eagle feathers and weasel fur and a bowl of Minnesota red clay. Roan Horse, following the instruction he had received last night, placed the pipe stem up on two forked sticks set in the ground.

Sticks came down on the drums and the dancing started again, the watchers shouting, the drummers singing, and the dancers wheeling in the steps of horses, antelope, eagles, and buffalo. They, too, shouted and blew on their eagle bone whistles, keening as their bodies swung through the hours, their eyes staring at the open circle above them even when the sun sat in it like a white coal. At a signal from Sitting Bull, the drums halted.

The ground was pink with paint that had run off with sweat. Roan Horse lifted the pipe from the sticks and all the other dancers took other, lesser pipes. In a long line, they all stepped to the drummers and offered the pipes to them. The drummers refused. They offered the pipes again and again were refused. On the fourth offer the drummers accepted the pipes for safekeeping while the dancers prepared for the next stage of the Sun Dance.

Sitting Bull and the other wichasha approached the dancers with sage and rubbed off the last of the red paint. Now they were painted with yellow for the power to grow. On their arms below their elbows and on their legs below their knees they were painted blue for the power to live and to destroy. On their backs they painted a half-moon. After he was painted, Roan Horse sang the first of the chants:

Father, paint the earth on me,
A nation I will make over.
A two-legged nation I will make holy.
Father, paint the earth on me.

The wichasha tied strips of buffalo hide around the dancers' ankles and wrists to give them stamina for the ordeal ahead. The dancers walked to the drummers and were offered their pipes. They refused three times and took them on the fourth, bringing them back to rest on their forked sticks. The sticks slammed down on the drumheads as all but two of the dancers milled with their yellow torsos and blue limbs around the tree. The other two stood with their eyes straight ahead as wichasha forced a sharpened awl through their breast muscles and fastened a heavy thong through the torn muscle. When the pain was too great, they threw their heads back to stare at the sun.

All around, the Lakota sang,

See where the sacred sun is walking!
In the blue robe of morning he is walking,
With his power greenward walking.
Hey-o-ha, hey-o-ha, hey-o-ha, hey-o-ha!

The two dancers leaned back on the thongs that fastened them through the tree to the sun. With their arms out, their chests full of song and eyes dry from staring, they flew around the tree. The pain freed them from the ground, raised them high above the other dancers, up to eagles, until with the sun setting they were cut loose and collapsed on the dirt.

All the other dancers would fly the same way over the next three days. The dancers were allowed neither food nor water, only some bark to chew on and wet their mouths. At night, outside the sweat bath lodge of the dancers, the men from the other nations talked, asking the Lakota the significance of one thing or another. The Inde accepted the dance without question; the men of the Savane saw it with scorn and awe. One thing was clear to all, and that was the pain that seemed to linger through the night from the bodies that crumpled to the ground each day.

"It is done to kill the proud heart," Sitting Bull explained to Black Horse. "There is a point when the hurt is too great. A man, no matter how brave, knows that he can stand no more. And yet he does."

"What does that mean?" Black Horse huffed.

"It means that he has been forced to place himself in the hands of Wakan Tanka. Then he can overcome anything. Pride is replaced by this knowledge, which is much more valuable."

"Huh," Black Horse said and licked the buffalo rib grease from his fingers at the same time he thought of the dancers in their lodge with stomachs two days empty. "What about this Where The Sun Goes," he asked to change the subject. "Has he done the Sun Dance?"

"He requested it and we allowed it. It was not easy for someone his age to do it for the first time."

"Where is he now? Why isn't he with us?"

"He is gone to the Great Salt Lake to see men who call themselves . . . Saints."

Only Roan Horse was left to swing on the fourth day. The visitors had bet money among themselves that no one could last and the losers were holding onto their pockets and saying that he had to actually dance on the thongs for a while before they'd pay. The Lakota were in their finest apparel, in bonnets of old men that streamed to the ground, women in soft buckskin dresses with bodices of intricate quill designs. The father of Roan Horse rode through the camp leading thirty stallions, giving them away to the poor in celebration of his son's honor.

The ones who had gone before and could still dance did so as the sun rose to the tree's circle. Their breasts were bound with *po-ipiye*, wild four o'clock, but they soon opened from the dancing. Roan Horse, the primary dancer, the last left and given a whole day to fly from the tree, was painted red with blue on his arms and legs. Eagle feathers were fastened to his wrists and in his undone hair. The wild, untamable roan horse of his vision was painted on his back. Everything was done to give him all the help he would need.

Sitting Bull walked to the sacred buffalo skull and filled all the sockets—eyes, jawbone, and ears—with sage. While he did so, he sang,

> *A sacred nation, they are appearing,*
> *They are appearing, may you behold!*
> *The bison nation, they are appearing,*
> *May you behold!*

As the last word ended, the sage blew from the skull on its mound. Sitting Bull picked up the heavy skull and ran a thong through the jaw, then he hung it around Roan Horse's neck so that it dangled down his back. Roan Horse's eyes found the sun overhead. With two firm, quick stabs, he ran the awl through the dancer's breasts and tied knots into the long leather bands. When the arms came down on the drums, Roan Horse let himself fall back, testing the thongs that tied him without escape to God.

As he swung around the tree, the buffalo skull pulling him to earth, his brothers and friends sang to him, thanking him for the honor he was doing them. By the time the sun had filled the circle and gone, all the Lakota were singing, praising the warrior whose courage was enough to honor his whole people. The figure they hailed was staggering, red under a red tree, his breast muscles bursting from his chest. His mind followed a handsome roan that galloped through the clouds.

He heaved back one more time and the thongs tore first one and then the other muscle out of his chest. The Lakota yelled with joy at the best feat a dancer could perform for his people. Black Horse felt his stomach sink into his groin. Sitting Bull and the other wichasha rushed out to bind the wounds. When a loser tried to pay off Stand Watie, he brushed him aside.

Roan Horse was back on his feet, his head bowed so that the skull could be taken from him. Sitting Bull pulled his face up so that he could see into the dancer's eyes. The Lakota smiled with pride as Roan Horse stood by himself, unassisted.

Sitting Bull led him away, out of the enclosure of the sacred tree and out toward a hill overlooking the camp and the river. All the Lakota and Tsitsistas, wichasha and watchers, spilled out after them, entirely surrounding the hill.

Waiting for Roan Horse and Sitting Bull on top of the hill was a stallion tethered to the ground. The pony had been painted blue and an eagle feather was braided into his tail.

"Do you need any help?" Sitting Bull asked softly.

"No, thank you, wichasha."

Roan Horse put his right hand on the horse's neck and swung himself over its back. He sat up and felt the weariness recede as if he were drawing new strength from the pony. Sitting Bull brought forth the sacred pipe that he had carried from the dancing ground and handed it to Roan Horse. The dancer took the pipe and rode out, rearing the pony, to each of the four winds, holding the pipe high as an offering and saying each time loud enough for all to hear, "Grandfather, you have given me this pipe and this morning star. Give me the eyes to see and the strength to understand, so that I may be a nation and live!"

>⫷⫸<

The television cables ran like whipsnakes along the hall to the conference auditorium. Inside electricians taped couplings for cameramen. The platform was so brightly lit that the Dog Soldiers and the members of the press they were surveying looked two-dimensional. Other Dog Soldiers were scattered throughout the auditorium, the hall, and near the embassy door. Everyone coming in was searched.

"This is the setting for a momentous news conference," the reporter from CBS said to her camera in the back of the auditorium. "Will you get a reading on that, Joe?"

While she waited, she taped some notes on the front of the camera. Liz Carney was a professional, in her thirties, chic with platinum hair and tweeds. "Okay?" The cameraman nodded.

"This is the setting for a momentous news conference. As reports of mobilization of the National Guard sweep the country, here in the capital a last-minute negotiator has arrived from the Indian Nation. Observers are puzzled. The president stated last night in a television address to the nation that he had offered to go anywhere, anytime to, as he put it, 'bring back new boundaries and an honorable peace to North America.' He said this offer was turned down by the Indians. So the sudden appearance here in this manner of the diplomat Holds Eagles has breathed new life into the speculation of possible negotiations and the peaceful redrawing of this continent.

"A fact sheet put out hastily by the Indian embassy says that Holds Eagles is twenty-eight years old, has served as a translator and as a special envoy to numerous countries. Indianologists admit that he is a new face but perhaps that's what this situation could use right now. Everyone agrees that the unknown negotiator will need more than a little luck to patch up relations between this country and his own after a century of mistrust and a growing climate of war fever."

In the hall the NBC man was taping his own introduction.

". . . can possibly resolve a situation in which ten million keep for themselves a tremendous area that is so desperately needed by our population of over two hundred million. Someone once said that Prussia was an army with a country. Today the Indian Nation is Prussia with leather shirts, trying to keep the continental heartland for itself with its publicized array of military technology. It's a little late in the day for Prussia to send us a Talleyrand." A director behind the camera waved and the newsman shrugged and ended again. "It's a little late for Prussia to start sending olive branches." The hand waved a second time. "It's a bit late in the day for the Indians to send us an olive branch. Christ."

"Strike the last word and tape it," the director said.

The educational network was filming in a corner. ". . . momentum can be stopped. The waves of violence that began growing in the sixties seem about to engulf us. The assassination of a president and of a candidate for president, the war in Vietnam, student protests, and, this year, the assassination of the Indian Chief of Nations Buffalo Rider, by an American—all these events seem to be accelerating to some sort of terrible crescendo. President Nielson met with members of his cabinet and the joint chiefs of staff late last night. The Indian Council of Chiefs has not yet elected its new leader and there is pressure on the president to act decisively before they do."

There were some laughs as a couple from the Liberation

Press came in. Their hair was mussed up and their faces flushed as usual from a run-in with the FBI on the street. They hunched against a wall to pull a pack of film from its hiding place inside a pair of pants.

"You'll just lose it on the way out," an ABC man called out.

The kids grinned and continued to load up. They would have lost everything if a Dog Soldier hadn't shown up in time. A DS came out now in his fringed jacket to say that the news conference was about to begin. The press took seats as close to the front as they could.

Two Indians came out and sat down at a table behind a low fence of microphones. The first, old, his face the shape and color of an avocado, was the *chargé d'affaires*, Bearman. The other was Holds Eagles. Their mismatched shadows were thrown onto the flag at their backs.

Bearman's little eyes darted around the auditorium and then he spoke.

"This conference has been called to give representatives of the American press an opportunity to hear a statement by an envoy of the Indian Nation. Texts of the statement will be available afterwards. There will also be a short question period. Holds Eagles."

There was no applause. Holds Eagles surveyed the Wasichu. One of the wire service reporters was the "importer" from Roanoke. As Holds Eagles continued to look at him, casually but deliberately, the intelligence man shifted uneasily and finally strode up the aisle as the reporters craned their necks to watch.

"I have come to the United States," Holds Eagles said, "to prevent a war no one can win. I wish that I could give the American people a list of new proposals at this time, but these are things that must be worked out in confidence between our two governments. All I can state is that I am in direct communication with the Council of Chiefs. The chiefs are anxious that the armies massed on our border never meet and that the missiles aimed at our cities are never fired. I would not insult your president by saying that he wants such a war. I would not insult the American people by saying that they want war. Neither do we. Let that be the basis of a new and lasting peace."

There was no applause. As the NBC director flipped on his walkie-talkie, a tiny voice inside it asked, "What did he say?"

"Nothing," the director said. He jabbed his newsman in the back with the sharp end of a pencil.

"What do you really hope to achieve with this trip, Mr. Eagles," the newsman said. "You come to an embassy that is run by a skeleton staff since most of them were recalled a week ago. Congress has already voted the president uses whatever powers he sees fit to protect American troops. Polls show that a majority of the American people back the president in demanding return of territories seized by your government. Doesn't your trip seem, honestly, an exercise in futility?"

"I hope not."

"What do you think of the phrase, 'Indian Giver'?" the Hearst man asked.

"It's a poor phrase."

"The United States has long had a number of sympathizers with the Red Man, people we call Pinks," the reporter persisted. "Do you plan to make contact with them?"

"I hope to make contact with the American people and their leaders."

One of the kids standing at the rear got Holds Eagles's attention. The boy spoke excitedly as his friend snapped the camera toward the table. "There have been rumors that the army, the FBI, and the Justice Department have been trying to prevent any agents from the Indian Nation from reaching Washington to start negotiations. That if you had not made it to the embassy, you would have been arrested and detained. Would you comment on this, please."

"I have no comment on that."

"Do you deny it?" It was Liz Carney.

"I have no comment."

She was about to pursue the point when the man from the *Daily News* asked whether Holds Eagles was aware that the last time an envoy came to Washington for eleventh-hour talks was just before Pearl Harbor.

"I hope that no attacks will be carried out by either side, now or later. If those are all the questions, ladies and gentlemen, thank you."

Holds Eagles made too fast an exit for any protests.

An hour later, President Nielson was rerunning a tape of the conference in the Oval Room. On the walls were television screens and more esoteric electronic equipment studded with dial locks. Surrounding all this was memorabilia of the Pacific, spears, machetes, wooden Polynesian shields. It was a big change from the lobster cages President Cabot had hung during the previous administration.

"What's with this having to sneak into Washington?" the president asked.

The attorney general, a rumpled, grey man in a matching suit, lifted his shoulder. "I don't know. He's just being cute. How come he didn't tell us he was coming?"

"Well, there's one thing for certain," the navy chief said, "he's stolen the march on us. This sets everything back."

"You'll have to talk with him, sir," the press aide said. "The networks gave him a pretty big play. I have a hundred requests for interviews."

"The bastard. I think we should go right ahead. We don't have forever," the attorney general said.

"Harry has a point. Talks can drag on forever," the national security man said. "A provocation on the border would put us back in the ballgame."

"I don't see why they can't be reasonable," the president said. "Why don't they just let us have the top half? There's plenty of room for them in the land that the pueblos take up now. We'd pay them for the rest."

There was an embarrassed quiet in the room. Nielson was a slight man with a long nose and cheeks that looked as if he'd been caught stuffing grapes in them. His lone distinction was in wiping out a Huk rebellion thirty years ago. Before becoming president he was the governor of California. Among the high-powered personalities in Washington, he tended to digress into equivocation and appeals for approval.

"That's Indians for you," the attorney general said finally. "They don't know a favor when they see it. As for provocation, I don't see how their missiles can be considered anything but a provocation. A gun at our head."

"You'll have to see him, sir," the press aide said. "Now that he's here. If you want to maintain your position vis-à-vis negotiation."

"Oh boy. Vis-à-vis. Let's kick the pipsqueak all the way to the border. He can join the Black Ass tribe," the attorney general muttered.

"And the interviews," the press aide went on. "How about those?"

"Pardon me, sir, but if there are going to be any interviews, I think we'd better check to see who's involved," the national security man said.

"Of course," the president said with decision. "We don't want this to turn into a propaganda circus."

The attorney general cleared his throat loudly.

"Harry?" the president asked.

"I just wanted to add that, of course, that's all this thing is. We've disallowed diplomatic channels to the Indians for weeks and their radio is thoroughly jammed. There's no way this character can send any messages back to the council or get any messages back. The whole thing is a slap in the face. That's what gets me angry."

"What about that?" the president turned to his press aide.

"A thought," the navy chief interrupted. "Let's say the talks start. No doubt Holds Eagles has a predetermined list of things he can say or not say. If we can somehow cause confusion in the set up, get them to deny what he says, then the talks will be exposed as a fraud and we can go ahead with a surplus of vindication."

"Not bad," the national security man said.

The president looked at the attorney general. Harry Moore had given the president advice for years, as a lawyer, a campaign manager, and now as head of the Justice Department.

"Sure," Moore said. "Meanwhile, I'll keep thinking."

That evening the press aide got up from the dinner table to answer the telephone. When he came back he was all grins.

"Harry Moore," he told his wife. "Gave the okay for Liz Carney on the Indian. She's not one of his favorites so I guess he's going along with my ideas of press relations. Not such a prick after all."

In the morning the streets were cleared by mounted police followed by trucks of sanitation workers with barriers. Pennsylvania Avenue, from the Hill to the White House, and all cross streets were lined with banners. Spectators arrived early and sat on the curbs with thermos bottles. Hot dog, balloon, flag, and ice cream vendors set up shop. The sound of bands warming up in the park drifted down the wide avenue. More spectators arrived, many in groups, patriotic associations vying for positions of prestige near the reviewing stand. Eagle Scouts lined up to guard the president's box with men from the Secret Service. The sidewalks were crammed with people now and the bands were louder. A roar went up. The president and his family were arriving in their limousine, and not far behind was Vice President Ho with his family. Former president Cabot took a seat of honor next to the president. Justices, governors, generals, admirals, senators, congressmen, a beloved comedian, a baseball Hall of Famer, cabinet members, and plainclothesmen rose and clapped as President Nielson waved with both hands. Immediately, the first band wheeled on to the street, stepping high between drums and clarinets to the bouncing baton of the drum major. The Marine Marching Band, the president's own, stepped smartly down to the president's box, and when it got there, broke into his favorite, "Clementine." The first of a hundred regiments came after it as the crowd cheered and waved flags and banners. One after another they strutted down the boulevard, snapping salutes at the reviewing stand. New York's Rainbow Division, the First Cavalry, bright middies from the Sixth Fleet, Philippine Freedom Fighters in their characteristic green scarves and berets, Samoan Rangers, Seabees, Chopper Champs, The Thunder Division, Leathernecks, Weekend Warriors, MP's getting goodhearted boos, the Seventh Fleet's Pacific Peacemakers, a float depicting the storming of Hamburger Hill, Navy Black Berets, Korean ROKs—each one snappier than the other until, when there seemed to be nothing left, the reviewing stand rose together for a standing ovation. A full complement of invalids in uniform and in company ranks was bringing up the end of the parade, with a major at its head, whipping off a beaut of a salute as he strode along on wooden stumps.

(The Vietnam War was finally won.)

Chapter Three

Nakaha un ampetu owihanke!
It's a great day for dying!

—Lakota

Captain Mills's scouts first found the trail of American Horse along Rabbit Creek. It was barely a hundredth the size expected, only a few tipis with old women setting out tanning poles. There was no need to share a victory as small as this. He led his renegades down on the camp without hesitating, rocks spilling from under the horses' hooves as the wide line scrambled down to the stream.

The squaws scattered like crows as the scouts splashed toward the village. Mills could see the old figure of American Horse running to a tipi with a scalp pole. The captain drew his service saber and headed for that tipi. There couldn't be more than thirty people in the whole camp, mostly female. It would be like one of the great old camp sweeps, like Sand Creek or Wounded Knee. The attack had barely reached the far bank when the front of American Horse's tipi fell away.

All of the tipis suddenly dismantled themselves. American Horse's and two others revealed gunners squatting behind the five barrels of a Gorloff. The others held men, no longer in squaws' dresses, firing repeaters.

It was early the next morning when Crook arrived at Rabbit Creek after a forced march through the night. The soldiers camped along the water in a mood of stupefied fatigue as the general rode up and down the site with MacKenzie and Dodge.

Crook was a religious man with a Bible in his saddlebag and a New Testament beard of long grey curls. No soldier cursed in the presence of this patriarch on his huge mule, Apache. No corrupt Indian agent even dared approach. General Crook regarded his work of domesticating the Indian as a task from the Lord. He was fanatically good.

"Beats me," MacKenzie said. He was walking his horse, kicking up stones. "Over a hundred men vanish into thin air."

Dodge halted before a wide stain of rusty ground. "Not completely," he said.

"All the scouts find is the trail of a small village, nothing that could tackle a force like Mills's. What could have happened?" MacKenzie said.

"What is the usual Indian tactic?" Crook asked.

"Ambush, naturally," MacKenzie said.

"That's what happened here. And it worked."

MacKenzie fingered his mustache. "Pardon me, General, but I don't see how. They would have needed Gatlings to pull something off like this."

"They had them," Crook said.

It was Dodge's turn to be skeptical. "I must say that Gatlings throw a hell . . . an awful lot of shells, General, and I hardly see any."

"They picked them up," Crook said.

"They picked up thousands of shells just so we wouldn't think they had Gatlings?" MacKenzie asked with disbelief.

"Exactly."

Colonel Dodge let out a long breath of air. "I must say that if that's the case, these reds are a lot smarter than I ever took them for." He and MacKenzie shared a look of bemusement.

"If that's what you'd say then you're starting to catch on," Crook said. He rode away on Apache, his beard fluttering in the early breeze. The general didn't stop until he was on top of a short butte overlooking the scene, alone.

It was plain what had happened. Mills and his men had stumbled across a small camp. Their luck was too good to pass up. One fast charge and they might even wind up with a chief in their bag. They had scrambled down a hill and the well-spaced tracks showed that they galloped to the river confidently. They probably were even allowed to get hold on the bank of the village because the ground there was torn up by careening horses violently trying to break their momentum. It was also where most of the blood was, like an official marker. Somehow, the Gatlings had been disguised up to that point. How many he couldn't tell, but perhaps as many as four.

Few of the attackers made it through the deadly village to the other side and they died there anyway. The rest, those who were alive, broke to the sides and straight back. Individual spots were located haphazardly in those directions, strawberry marks on the ground. So Mills and his scouts, veteran fighters, had dropped from the face of the earth.

A Pawnee scout rode up the butte to Crook.

"Nan-tan Lupan, we found the grave," the Indian said.

The two of them rode up the creek about a hundred yards. A group of scouts stood along the bank with shovels. At their feet was a litter of flesh, what was left of bodies that had been hacked into several parts. Even the mercenaries seemed stunned. Crook got off his mule. He took the Bible from his bag and flipped familiarly to the Valley of Death. The Pawnee said some things in their own language.

"It is as you said," the head scout said. He was a white man named Frank North, a major who dressed as the Indian he had become in twenty years of living with the Pawnee nation, marrying a squaw and living on buffalo. "They took the bodies and buried them to scare the rest of the scouts. They mutilated the bodies and put them in the river so that even if they were found we'd know that their souls had gone to the water devils. It's not good."

Crook's eye traveled up the bank. He could see now that most of it had been used as a mass tomb, though the loose earth of the creek's edge had been the cleverest way of concealing it.

"Want us to dig the rest up?" North asked.

"No, Major. Put these back where you found them. Place a small marker where no one is likely to find it. Tell your men not to talk about this with anyone, as an order from me."

North motioned the scouts to bury the bodies. "Anything else, sir?"

"Yes. I want sharp men stationed beyond the sentries tonight. You can get them for me, can't you?"

The troops were beginning to stir for food when Crook came back to his tent. The encampment was on the other side of the river from where the fight had been, the foot soldiers lying beside the triangle of their stacked Springfields, the horse soldiers on their stomachs and saddles near the tethering lines of horses. The Indians always camped apart. For some reason, the Almighty had seen fit to make both the white man and the Indian intolerant of each other's smell. The ways of the Lord were mysterious.

In his tent, General Crook fell asleep for the first time in thirty-two hours. The sound of his wagons and artillery rolling into the camp was comforting.

Frank North was riding. He had been the man to spot the strange signs at Rabbit Creek the day before. His wide, tanned face was taut with weariness and fright. The bodies in the creek had been a very bad sign. Nothing like that had ever happened to scouts before. To soldiers, yes, but not to scouts. He was too much Pawnee not to feel a dread.

Now he'd heard that the Crows were in the area. Two hundred of them under Alligator and Stand-up were supposed to have joined the rest of the scouts already, the way they always did. For them to sit silently without meeting Crook was queer. Crows loved nothing more than fighting the Lakota.

The word was true. North and his brother-in-law discovered the Crow camp ten miles to the west. A pair of warriors rode out to meet them. They greeted the squawman and the Pawnee as usual, shaking their left hands, but North couldn't keep his eyes off the Crow rifles, brand new Winchester Repeaters.

Alligator and Stand-up received North in the latter's tipi. Alligator made the more brilliant appearance, his hair dressed with dyed horse tails. Stand-up was the one who made the decisions. The fact that he was letting Alligator do all the talking was not right. North decided to bring the issue to a head by lying.

"The fact is," he said, "Nan-tan Lupan is wondering why you do not quit this camp for his own. He says that it would be much easier to make plans for fighting if you were with him."

Alligator shut up. Stand-up called to someone outside the tipi. A young woman came in. She was beautiful and modest, dressed in the fashion that Crow women were famous for, a red line painted in the part of her black hair and a buckskin dress decorated with what must have been three hundred elk's teeth.

"This is my new wife," Stand-up said. "Why would I want to leave her and go fighting? Only a crazy man would do that. I think I will rest for a while and let the Wasichu do his own fighting, if he can."

"And you, Alligator?"

"I will stay with my friend."

The conversation seemed to have come to a dead halt. North had fought next to Stand-up and knew there was no forcing his hand, but he felt he had to get something more.

"Let me ask you something Stand-up. You don't have to answer if you don't want. Do you trust me?"

The Crow nodded his head. He knew it was a serious question, so he thought. "Do I trust you? Pehin hanska has asked me to trust him. Father Washington has asked me to trust him. Pahuska, Buffalo Bill, has asked the same thing, and Nan-tan Lupan. But you ask if I trust you. As much as I have trusted any Wasichu, I do trust you. It is because you are just a little bit like us."

North realized that they were talking on an entirely new level. A Wasichu would not have known it but, as Stand-up said, he was no longer entirely white.

"Then let me ask you again," he said. "You will not fight for a while?"

"I promise," Stand-up said, "I will not fight for a while."

As he left the Crow camp, Frank North was sure that every warrior he saw had a new rifle.

General Crook and his staff were angled over a map. With his finger, Crook drew trench lines for the night's encampment. He ordered double sentries and the dispatching of flares.

"Begging your pardon, sir," MacKenzie said, "but the men are awfully tired from last night's march and I've never known hostiles to attack at night."

Crook leaned on his arms patiently. "Indeed, General. Do you think they're afraid of the dark?"

"No, it's just I . . ." MacKenzie trailed off in a fluster.

"I want the supplies in the very center of the camp, not at the periphery," Crook went on. "That's what Crazy Horse is going to go for, the same way he did at the Rosebud, supplies and horses. Major Gordon, you've had experience with Gatlings. Set them up with overlapping fields of fire with men who can stay awake. By the way, some of North's men will be posted out beyond the regular sentries. If they see anything, they will fire three shots. Try not to get any of our own Indians. That's all, gentlemen. General, I'd like you to stay for a second. I need your help for tomorrow's assignments."

The rest of the officers trooped out. MacKenzie was happy to feel of enough importance to stay.

"What about tomorrow, sir?" he asked when they were alone.

"Nothing," Crook said. He sat down on his folding chair and asked MacKenzie to take the other one. "I wanted to talk about our present situation, Mac. I don't necessarily feel that we're sure to be attacked tonight, you'll be happy to know. But I think it's a real possibility. In case we are and something happens to me I'd like you to have the best chance of getting out of here, since you'll be in command."

MacKenzie's mouth gaped a little. "Get out, sir? Why, they'd never attack us. Anyway, we're far too powerful."

He waited to be interrupted. "Go on," Crook said.

"We're the biggest army force in this area in years. We have artillery, Gatlings, modern support, and crack soldiers. Right now, we control this whole area just by being here," MacKenzie said. He waited for Crook's reply like a student waiting for a grade.

"Fine," Crook said. "Now, let me give you a slightly different rendering of the same facts. The Indian's viewpoint. Tell me how you like it.

"We are a force of about two thousand men, horse, food, and support, against a cavalry of at least ten thousand. Our big advantages over this enemy are our discipline, tactics, and superior weapons, artillery, et cetera. Suppose we didn't have those advantages. Then we are simply an army outnumbered five to one. What happened here yesterday gives us reason to think twice about each of those categories.

"Or consider the fact that four hundred of our men are Indians. Our best men at fighting with knowledge of the country. We lost one hundred of those men yesterday, perhaps without taking one life in return. What was done to those dead men might have been an effort to dissuade the rest of the scouts from serving with us. Then we'd be a crippled army, outnumbered more than six to one."

MacKenzie stared out the tent, across the creek to where the village had been. "I never thought of it that way," he said.

Crook paused a moment, then slapped his second on the back. "Cheer up, Mac, that's a deliberately black picture I painted, and I doubt very much that the Good Lord has abandoned our cause so completely. I just want you to have these possibilities in mind in case of the unexpected."

MacKenzie was an optimist at heart and he immediately smiled with relief. He half wished that the general was a drinking man so they could damp the phantoms in a more companionable style.

"The evidence that they have machine guns is far from proof that Crazy Horse is going to turn up with a battery of artillery," Crook went on. "Their tactics will remain primitive simply because they are a primitive people. As for the Indians who have served under me, I've never been betrayed. Down in Arizona, against Geronimo, I had Navaho, Pima, Pueblo, some Yaqui from Mexico, and even some Apache. Pawnee have never given me any trouble. Stand-up's Crow are a little late but they'll be showing up any day now and we'll be back at strength. As Christians we have to keep in mind that there are good Indians too."

Crook's soldiers went to sleep as the sun and the temperature went down. Over their shoulders they pulled moth-eaten greatcoats. In their stomachs lay beans soaked with vinegar to kill the taste of rot. They lay with their heads toward their carbines. In their back pockets were knuckle dusters lined with nails. Civil War veterans, German and Irish immigrants, refugees from prison and families and civilization took a perverse pride in their servitude.

Lieutenant Bryan Starr was a Fenian, convicted by the English of murder, who had come with a thousand more of his countrymen when the Union was buying brigades for the war. He'd stayed in and one out of every three dollars he earned went to the Irish cause. The fact that one after the other of the charity's collectors in New York had absconded with the funds did not deter him from finding another. To stop sending the money would have been to admit that he never would see Ireland again.

Starr was looking up at the prairie night when the first grenade went off directly overhead. Others followed in rapid succession, falling in a line to the supply wagons in the center of the camp. The sky lit up with flares amid the shouts and random shots of sentries. The grenades fell with seeming ineffectiveness into the ammunition until one wagon exploded like an enormous Roman candle, wheels and shells spinning in a burst through the troopers stationed by it. As more soldiers ran to help, the corral was thrown open and the horses driven out to run through the ranks of men trying to wake up and load their rifles at the same time.

Crook raced through the camp with Dodge, rallying the men. The sentries pulled in on a signal from the bugler as flares continued to light the ground. North was dispatched to round up the horses. Sergeants made a rapid count of their squads. The Gatling teams withdrew to the main body without having fired a shot. Rifles were issued to the teamsters while the surgeon examined Lieutenant Starr and placed a pair of silver dollars on his eyes. Guns at the ready, the expeditionary force of the United States waited for the attack.

When the sun came up they were still waiting, red eyes squinting over sights at an empty plain. Cooks walked along the lines distributing bacon and hard bread. The officers rode to where Crook commanded on the crest of a butte. Frank North was with the general. The staff wore an air of triumphant resolution.

"You were right, sir," General MacKenzie said. "Looks like they changed their minds, though."

The sun shined into their faces, gilding them generously with its newness. Major Royall poured water from his canteen down the back of his neck. Motes rose from the shuffling of the horses.

"The situation?" Crook asked.

"Better than we first thought," Dodge said. "One man killed, twenty casualties, about five of them serious. We lost about fifteen horses and one wagon. The main thing we lost was a night's sleep," he ended with a smile.

"What I don't get is how they got so many men into the camp," MacKenzie said as an afterthought. Crook looked at North.

"They didn't," North said. "Only one man had to come in, probably wading in the creek, to free the horses." He held up the blackened stub of an arrow. "The grenades came in this way."

The officers looked at the shaft incredulously, the chuck of a grenade still strapped to it.

"They didn't have to get too close," North said. "With a sinew-backed bow, you can shoot an arrow clear through the chest of a buffalo." He flicked the striped turkey feather fletches. "Cheyenne."

"How far?" Dodge asked.

"Seventy-five yards, at least. Any Indian worth his moccasins can do that, get in that close and shoot that far," North said.

"You sound like you sort of admire it," Dodge said.

"I admire it," Crook said. "It gives them the most mobile artillery in the world. If this were a tactical problem, gentlemen, what would you do about it?"

"Post more sentries," Captain Henry said.

"Trip wires," suggested another officer.

"Why not set up Gatlings like last night but have them shoot at random intervals," Dodge said.

"Fine," Crook said. "Now, perhaps you have some ideas of why we're receiving grenades in the night without an attack. Colonel?"

"The only explanation is that we scared them off," Dodge said. "They sure aren't going to waste the few grenades they can get their hands on just to keep us awake."

"That depends, doesn't it?" Crook said.

"On what, sir?"

"On if they have their hands on only a few."

An hour after sunrise, North's scouts rode in. The area was clean. Crook had the buglers sound "saddle up." As the camp turned to the business of changing from fixed arms to arranging its long caravan, General Crook retired alone to his tent to write in his diary:

> The order has been given for the army to move in a
> sweep as a clearing action. Actually, we will arrive

at the Red Cloud Indian Agency in two weeks, God willing. Our situation has shifted dangerously from that of an offensive force to a besieged defensive one. This cannot be tolerated despite the general ignorance of this position. The hostiles are receiving a large amount of weapons that are, in some cases, superior to our own. Until that flow is interdicted, no victory will be achieved. I am sure that the Indian Ring that George Custer revealed at this agency is behind our problem. I will ask our friendly Indians there to help us end the insurrection at the same time.

Maj. N. says that the Crows are reluctant to join us. Odd.

He wrote a confidential assessment of the situation and gave it to a pair of Shoshone to deliver to army headquarters on a steamboat cruising the Yellowstone River. When it was received, a fresh formation of cavalry was equipped under the command of General Miles at Fort Keogh. It was the last heard from the army under Crook for more than three weeks.

Every night, the attacks were predictable, unavoidable. The "mosquito bites," as Dodge first called them, were only an annoyance at first. Then the expedition found itself marching without sleep, riding horses that had no rest, against a still-unseen enemy. In time they became an army without confidence, pushing one foot ahead of the other behind ambulances now filled with wounded. Still, Crook pushed them on in his growing certainty that only a descent on the Red Cloud Agency could end the torment. Puffy faced, many of the cavalry were on foot for lack of mounts. Their revenge for Custer was long forgotten. All they cared for was rest or to leave completely the

"Great American Desert." Many of the troopers who patrolled the camps at night were asleep on the necks of their mounts.

On the eighteenth day the Plains itself struck. The afternoon was hot and airless as usual. The soldiers, marching double time, breathed through cracked lips and saw through swollen eyelids. Then it changed. The wind, when it blows, blows harder on the Plains than anywhere else in America, and when winter comes it comes on the wind. The first blow of the winter of 1876 met the men of Crook and MacKenzie with an arctic blast. Those who could see saw the sky turn blue, then black. Into their faces the wind came on stronger, the temperature dropping a degree every thirty seconds. Before Crook could reach the lead company, it was below freezing and a full blizzard was engulfing them. Sergeants ran along the line screaming for the soldiers to halt. When some men tried to start fires, the wind threw the flames into their faces. The surgeons in the ambulances fought to close the curtains and cover the wounded with buffalo skins. In a short time, the grand army that had started out a month ago could hardly be seen.

If it had not been for the strain of the infuriating attacks of the past weeks, the rumors that Red Cloud's agency was behind them, and then the final test of the blizzard, Crook might have been able to control his army when it finally pulled into the old warrior's reservation. As it was, one out of five of the troopers were casualties from heat stroke, frostbite, or grenades, and the rest were ravaged. Only Crook's stern faith had kept them in order so long. That and their determination to kill Indians, any Indians.

Red Cloud was determined on peace. The chief who had led the wars of the sixties, who spoke at Cooper Union and the White House, the pet of European philosophers, rode out on a white horse without his quiver to meet the army. Crook was an old friend, an honorable man who regarded him in the same light. There would be no more unwinnable wars for the Indians if the impressive Lakota could help it.

The meeting took place on a meadow west of the reservation. A stream ran along one side of it. It was beside this stream that the Pawnee scouts stood witness.

Colonel Dodge was the first officer to meet Red Cloud in the middle of the meadow. The chief asked to be taken to Nan-tan Lupan. Dodge proceeded to arrest him, a move highly popular with the beaten soldiers. North arrived and protested, as did the Pawnee. The soldiers were pretty certain by now, though, that they had been deliberately misled by the scouts during the whole march. They would not again be taken by any filthy Indian or squawman. They especially resented that the Pawnee, trained from birth to fight the winds of the Plains, had suffered little during the storm. A squad of dismounted cavalry, acting on its own, placed North under arrest.

Crook arrived and the situation seemed less tense. The general said that the chief, head of twenty thousand amicable Sioux, had come as a friend and ordered him released. Dodge let him go. North was also released. Crook apologized but told Red Cloud that he would have to have all the Sioux called in to the agency and searched, and that all arms would be confiscated. He explained that he was forced to do this because of a flow of arms to hostiles through the agency. Red Cloud answered that if arms were moving through the agency, the agency should be inspected, not quiet Indians. He would also appreciate it, he said, if the inspection would investigate why they had to pay three times the price for cornmeal that whites paid. As for the arms, the treaties Red Cloud had signed at the end of his fighting guaranteed the right to keep arms to shoot game. Without game they would starve.

Crook said that he would allow those Indians to keep their arms who would join him in bringing in their brothers on the warpath. Then they could hunt all the game they wanted. He said, as an old friend, that this was the only course they had open to prove that the reservation policy could work, otherwise the soldiers would have to round up all the Indians. Red Cloud said that he would have to discuss something as important as this with the Shirtwearers, his council of chiefs. If he did not the people would not agree to what was decided. Crook said that he must have his answer the same day.

Red Cloud pulled the reins on his horse and started back to his camp. The sight of the chief, the man they believed responsible for their grief, heading away scot free was too much for some of the troopers of the Fifth Regiment. Crook saw the rifles being raised but it was too late. Red Cloud's back burst under the fusillade of shots, blood mottling the rump of his horse as he slumped off onto the ground. Frank North ran out with his hands up to stop the firing and he was shot down too. The white horse ran away, riderless, to the Lakota camp. The Pawnee along the stream jumped to their ponies and raced off in shock. It was not unusual for a parley under truce to end in this fashion but no other betrayal in American history had as much effect as the one on Red Cloud's Meadow beside Squawman's Creek.

General Crook, through sheer force of personality, had the murderers put under arrest by their reluctant comrades. A fast war conference was called among the officers by Crook. The consensus, led by Dodge, was that their only move now was immediate attack on Red Cloud's camp before the irate Indians left to join Sitting Bull and doubled the enemy's ranks, a preemptive stroke. Crook finally saw that to turn back would dissolve his forces. The attack was ordered.

By this time the white pony had carried its message to Red

Cloud's camp. In case there was any mistake, a Pawnee rode in soon after with a full description of the killing. It took only minutes for women and children and old people to get together their few things and start out to the Plains on foot, horse, and travois. Outlying camps were warned by callers. The first word at the agency came as Lakota broke through the door and stripped the traders of rifles and bullets.

In the camp rudimentary defenses were being constructed. Trenches were dug and breastworks made of the loose dirt. Men took out their magic shields and performed their medicine as quickly as they could. Stretched out along a river, the camp resembled a long neck that could be chopped off a bit at a time. Since most of Red Cloud's followers were out hunting to store up for the winter or in farther camps, the defenders consisted of two thousand warriors spread thin.

As Major Gordon led the first phalanx of cavalry upstream of the camp, a rider was circulating among the defenders. It was the Teton Lakota, White Bull, who had killed Custer. He told the Shirtwearers that Crook's was not the only army in the buttes nearby. They Fear His Horses, the man they had called renegade, was close with enough warriors to erase the Wasichu. He would not spend those warriors to save them, though, if they were only going to go back to obeying the men who had killed Red Cloud. The Shirtwearers had to declare themselves for Sitting Bull.

George Crook, Nan-tan Lupan, drew up before the village with an ache in his heart. He had hoped to bring the Indians in peacefully after one quick victory. The saving of souls was the real work of a Christian and he had hoped to do it with his sword and his book. At this moment another village came to mind, a Cheyenne camp of twelve years before, at Sand Creek. Another religious man, Colonel J. M. Chivington, a Presbyterian elder from Denver, had asked the Indians to camp along the creek to show their good intentions. Chivington had then given the order to "Kill and scalp all Indians! Big and little—scalp them all! Nits make lice!" Chivington, the man he despised most on this earth, who rode down the babies for sport and took the scalps himself, was the man he would be copying. When all was in order, he gave the word to attack.

Gordon dashed down to the river with four companies of horse troopers as the bugle sounded. Teams drove wagons with Gatlings to the ends of the camp. MacKenzie's three cavalry companies hit the water. The orders of the two forces were to ride through the camp and then back towards the river, catching the Sioux as they came out of their tipis, pushing them to the water. Dodge's infantry started wading across to meet the survivors. The few scouts that were left, mostly Shoshone under Washakie and a ragtag group under Rowland, served as Crook's reserves.

Gordon, his saber circling in the air, led his men in a leap over the right breastworks. The Sioux fired up at them and more fire came from the trenches, but only a few of the troopers fell as, screaming with excitement, they swept through the fires and hides and tipis unloading their revolvers. The defenders on the left side buckled under MacKenzie's charge even though many of the soldiers rode through with their chests festooned with arrows. Using their swords, they slashed the tipi poles so that they collapsed on the men inside. Others dragged the tipis into fires to set them blazing. When the two charges had passed through, the village was a scene of crawling men, fallen horses, and smoking hides. MacKenzie and Gordon joined and came back toward the river. The Sioux in the trenches turned to face them, ignoring the infantry coming at their backs. In the moment before the horses swept toward them again, the Indians began chanting their death songs, "It is better to die gloriously doing brave things than to die an old man! Better to die, better to die!"

MacKenzie, panting, sweat and blood matting his hair, hatless from a grazing bullet, stood up in his stirrups to shout the charge when he noticed new horsemen, not Gordon's, at his rear. After a moment of confusion he was relieved to see that they were the Pawnee scouts. Then he saw the Sioux with them, and Crazy Horse. More warriors appeared from the brush in tens and hundreds.

Crook had seen the enemy before MacKenzie and Gordon and was himself leading the reserves through the water on the Apache. The only defendable location was the village. That was where his men were.

The Pawnee and Lakota drove the cavalry back through the camp to the river. The infantry, gaining its foothold on the camp's bank, couldn't fire for fear of hitting their own men. Crook rallied his horse troopers at the tipis, wisely leaving the last wiping up to his foot soldiers. He ordered sergeants to take fagots and burn every tipi left standing. Then, under withering fire from the superior repeaters, he took his cavalry in an orderly retreat back to the trenches. There with the gutted camp on one side and the river on the other, he resolved to take his stand.

Crazy Horse moved the Indians back to dismount and gather fresh ammunition. Sliding on their stomachs, they came within fifty yards of the soldiers. Anything that showed its head above defenses lost it. Among the wounded and hobbled horses, Crook made his battle plans. Gordon and Rowland were dead and Dodge was dying, propped against the carcass of a horse. Half of the ranks were dead or wounded. A ring of Shoshone under Washakie served as Crook's bodyguard.

"Stay," MacKenzie urged. "We've got water and we'll never make it out of here with the wounded. We'd hardly make it out anyway," he said between gulps from his canteen. He pushed the canteen onto Washakie but the Shoshone looked away.

"Have to get out," Crook said. "A hundred and fifty supply wagons out there waiting for Crazy Horse to find. And if we stay here another day, none of us will get out ever."

"The wounded," MacKenzie said in horror.

"Will have to stay here mostly. They'll be slaughtered and mutilated but my soul has already gone to hell. I have to save those I can." His voice was hoarse and splintery from yelling during the retreat and he could hardly be heard.

The soldiers made their break at dusk. Flares were thrown toward the Indians to confuse them as saddled troopers opened fire in volleys. If they had moved a minute later, it would have been too late. The captured Gatlings were just being loaded.

Because the remaining wounded were firing, too, the Indians hesitated. It was enough for Crook to lead six hundred survivors in a gallop along the bank and into the water. The first of them fell during the dark fording. Meanwhile the Lakota under Gall waited for them on the other side. In the shadows of the trees the two cavalries met, striking out with sabers and lances, revolvers and bows. The first wave of troopers was cut down, but the others forced their way through the Indians up the butte and onto the plain in a desperate race to the wagons.

The teamsters heard the shots a mile away as the fight moved toward them. Lashing out with twenty-foot whips they drove the wagons into circles and dove under them with their guns. The artillery that Crook had left behind was loaded and fired, shells arching over the troopers into the Indian horses. As MacKenzie reached the wagons he ordered them out of their circles and to get moving.

They drove the wagons over the moonlit plains in what must have seemed a war at sea, as teamsters fired their tiny two-pound cannons over the endless swells of grass at a faintly seen adversary. The crippled wagons and wounded fell back to be swallowed in the night. When the 422 troopers, 190 drivers, and 100 wagons entered the palisades of Fort Laramie, they ended the longest running battle of the Indian Wars. Crook was not one of them. He had fallen early, near the 482 soldiers dead in the trenches and tipis, his body lying in the river that bears his name, Grey Fox's Creek.

>►◄◄

"What does this mean?" President John Taylor asked from his throne overlooking the Empire of Deseret.

John Setter rose from his chair and stood in front of the large map that filled one wall of Taylor's office. Mormon elders waited with poorly concealed excitement. Setter's delegation of Banakwut and Kadohadacho were better at hiding their glee.

"It means," Setter said, drawing his hand in a wide sweep over the map, "that the United States has ceased to be the authority over this land. They are only a party to the struggle, the losing party."

Taylor looked down at the reports on his desk once more. The rout of Crook's expedition. The rising of Indians across the frontier. It would be easy, he knew, so easy to assume that the Revelations were coming true, that the word of Mormon was coming to pass as Joseph Smith had promised.

"It is God's hand writ large," Orson Pratt said. "The Gentiles have been thrown back by the Lamanites. It is the Judgment of God, the test that brings the Indians, the Sons of Laman, son of Lehi, back to grace. Why do we hesitate?"

All the same, President Taylor hesitated. Pratt was a proselytizer, the man responsible for the conversions among the Lamanites, a visionary. It did not pay for the president of Deseret to be so quickly swayed. He took another look at the map. At one time almost all of it, from Mexico to Canada and from California to the Mississippi, had been claimed by Deseret. The United States had forced the Mormon hand back to the Department of Utah. The Gentiles had killed Joseph Smith in Illinois. Brigham Young, the man he had succeeded, believed that the Lamanites, despite their fall to a life of dissolution, would rise victorious to Mormon and Moroni with a new Revelation. But would the new Revelation come from a Lamanite like the barely literate Wovoka? Could there actually be common cause between savages and the Latter-Day Saints who walked the wide streets of Salt Lake City? Could the Indians really hold back the United States Army when Mormon's own army, the Nauvoo Legion, had failed?

"Tell me," Taylor said. "Tell me what a white man like yourself, Mr. Setter, is doing in this war? What's in it for you?"

Setter folded his arms. "It's very simple, President Taylor. I am not white; I am Indian. Mandan. It is a trait among the Mandan for many to be born with paler skin and lighter hair. Albinism, some say."

His statement fell with the force of a Revelation on the Mormons. "That explains it," Pratt exclaimed. "A Mandan, one of the last Sons of Nephi, as Brigham Young . . ."

"Enough," Taylor warned. "Revelations are coming a little hot and heavy right now. You don't have to tell anyone here the thoughts of President Young on the inhabitants of this country. For some reason, I think that the last person you have to tell is our guest, Mr. Setter." He turned back to Setter. "A Mandan, huh? Just happen to be one of the few descendants of Nephi alive? Very impressive. Are you a Mormon, Mr. Setter? I see your friends here, the Bannock and Caddo, have all been converted by the good Elder Pratt. But are you?"

"No," Setter said.

"Then why should we believe you; can you tell me that, Mandan or no Mandan?"

"You will have to choose who you will believe. The Gentiles or us. All I am telling you is that you will have to choose very soon."

Setter's party was ushered out so that the president, theocratic dictator of forty thousand souls, could commune with God. Pratt was with them, showing them the wonder of the City of Zion. It was a marvel. Large buildings rose in a crescendo to the huge tabernacle, a mountain in the sky. Lombardy pines bordered the street eight rods wide. All was set out as prophesied by Isaiah, Ezekiel, Revelations, and the Book of Esther.

"Don't worry," Pratt said enthusiastically, "President Taylor will see the light. It's just that he did not have the experience of accompanying Brigham to the Rio Grande Valley and finding the ruins of the Ho-ho-kam, your ancestors. Oh, there was no doubt in Brigham's mind that the children of the bad brother Laman would be brought back to the path of Mormon. I don't think he could help being impressed by the fact that you are a son of Nephi and Moroni." He rubbed his hands. "Oh, these are great days for all but the Gentiles."

"What about the New Dispensation?" one of the Caddo asked.

"A new Revelation would dispose of that and your Wovoka has the new Revelation."

The large Mormon families gaped as the Indians, Lamanites or not, strolled through their boulevards.

President Taylor was finished communing with God and was communing with the head of the Sons of Dan, the Mormon secret police. It was Taylor's turn to walk in front of the great map.

"Fort Lemhi in Idaho," he said to his one-man audience.

"Fort Bridger and Fort Supply in Wyoming. Moab in east Utah," he went on, pointing at each one. "San Bernardino in California, Genoa in Nevada. An empire seven hundred miles wide, that's what Brigham Young set out as the limits of Deseret, limits from the Book of Mormon. I remember what he said in '47. He said, 'Give me ten years and I shall ask no odds of the United States.'" He stopped for breath, seeing on the map the thousand fertile, irrigated towns of the Mormon dream.

"Now look at us. Robbed of all but a quarter of our land by Gentiles, the same murderer who killed Joseph Smith and Hyrum Smith too. With a so-called governor put over us. And you know what he's going to do; he's going to call us out as militia to fight these Indians because we're going to be the only army around here pretty soon."

"That's what he's going to do," the Danite agreed. "Any day now." He was a burly man with a grizzled beard that grew from the underside of his chin. As a young man he had been blessed by the Prophet and told that no bullet could harm him. In battles with the state militia in Illinois, Ohio, and Missouri and in fights with Indians throughout Deseret, none ever had.

"All right," Taylor said. "Brigham was a great man, a great apostle, a saint. But most of all he was a practical man. Who do you think is going to win this thing? Have the Indians got a chance?"

The Danite crossed his legs to help him think. "Well, President Taylor, a week ago I would have said not a Chinaman's chance, if you'll excuse the expression. Today, today, I'd have to say yes. Very remote, but now there's no doubt that they have a chance.

"If you'll remember all those breeds coming down from Canada that I told you about with arms. Now they have half the supplies that Crook started out with. So they're pretty well set up. As for reinforcements, they've got more every day. I don't know what the army thinks they're up against, but my estimate, with Red Cloud's band, is at least fifty thousand. And friends. Someone in Canada is running the show, I'm sure, with the English in back of the whole shindig."

"This man Setter hints at that sort of thing but he won't say for certain until we commit ourselves his way," Taylor said.

"I shouldn't think so. At any rate, the way things are right now, the army will win. For one thing, we're going to be sent out along with every other settler in the territory to go Indian hunting. I don't care how good these Indian generals are; they'll break. In time, they'll break." He hunched his shoulders together. "Of course, we're going to be right in the middle of it and there are going to be a pile of dead Mormons before they break."

"And Washington will just step over the corpses and take the City of Zion away from us like they've tried before."

"It's a dilemma, sir," the Danite said sympathetically.

"Perhaps." Taylor sat down. "Let us say, for purposes of speculation, what effect we might have if we joined the rebellion. Don't play games with me, friend, I know the thought has occurred to you."

A grin split the Danite's cherubic face. "Fifty-fifty. With the Nauvoo Legion, yes, fifty-fifty."

"And who would you work with, for curiosity's sake?" Taylor asked.

"The Dog Soldiers is a sort of police society that operates in many of the large Plains tribes," the Danite said shyly. "How do you think you would like working with Sitting Bull?"

"I . . ." Taylor searched the right words out of his heart, "I can't help but believe that there is some responsibility on us to fulfill the prophecy of the return of the Lamanites. If we don't, who will?" he said sincerely.

Setter, the Kadohadacho and Banakwut, and the Council of Twelve reconvened in Taylor's office. The president had his head buried in his hands as they took their seats. The Indians nudged each other in respect for that fact that the Mormon had been talking with God. Taylor sighed deeply and sat up, his face drawn with exhaustion.

"I have not yet reached a decision," he said dramatically. "But I would like to hear more about the visions of Wovoka."

It would be easy to say that it was Wovoka's vision that changed the course of history. Or the heroism of They Fear His Horses, or the wisdom of Sitting Bull. Certainly, European capital and the Church of the Latter-Day Saints were eager to play their parts. But it was John Setter, Where the Sun Goes, who was the single most important figure, for he had the genius to bring all these factors together.

When Setter rode away from Salt Lake City, he knew well enough that he alone had set the accepted myths of history ajar. "To presume that it couldn't be done," he wrote later, "was a presumption based more on racial conceit than fact. It took no brilliance on my part, only the ability to see simple matters.

"The British said that the Americans were mentally incapable of carrying out their revolution. They called them pettifogging lawyers, riotous mechanics, disorderly farmers, and lawbreaking merchants. Also, that a war would destroy the upper class, and no country, they said, could function without that. Washington was the simple man who understood the mechanics of the war he had to fight. If the colonies could maintain their unity, pick only battles they could win, win public opinion abroad, and hang on, they would hold the British at a standstill. The point was that the Americans would win any standstills because it was their country.

"During the Indian Wars, the Americans took the other role. Despite the fact that the Plains nations were engaging in climactic jacquerie, that the Indians had numerous war veterans, lawyers, farmers, and merchants to draw on across the continent if they could be motivated, that leadership among the nations was at a remarkably high level, the United States assumed that we were mentally incapable of carrying out a successful struggle for freedom. It was an attitude that persisted for twenty years after the last Wasichu soldier was driven over the Missouri. It was such a monumental conceit—I can still see it on President Taylor's face—that I have always approached it with a good deal of awe."

Setter was ten years old when wicranran crept through the earthen lodges of the Mandan. The epidemic struck down people as they stood cooking food, as they loaded furs into boats, as they buried their dead. In but a few days, the Mandan cliffs over the river were littered with bodies as if by the wrath of some vengeful god. The plague moved west, destroying the Hidatsa Nation first and tainting a dozen others as the germs diffused in the prairie winds.

No one dared approach the Mandan villages. Certainly not the white traders who for fifty years had made the easy voluptuosity of Mandan girls legend. For the Jesuits, however, there were other lures. The Society of Jesus had been operating in the woods of North America for more than two hundred years, a different kind of Canadien Service that ferried souls instead of furs. The annals of Jesuit Relations were and continue to be the fullest analysis of Indian life ever compiled. The last of the Mandan people called for a priest.

Father Mercure arrived ten days after the disease lapsed from the village. He would have arrived sooner, but the breeds paddling his canoe would not go near the village. Instead, filthy kerchiefs wrapped around their faces and reeking of garlic, the scouts, in their haste to get away, left the Frenchman among the round Mandan boats which were tangled in the underbrush along the banks. Some were empty and some had puffy, black arms hanging over the wales. As he walked under the cliff that the main camp stood on, he experienced a void inside that he would never have believed could exist, that almost drew his faith away like a flame in a vacuum. The vultures made a dark, curling cloud in the sky. Along the edge of the cliff others were hopping, too glutted to rise. Along the bottom of the cliff were the picked bodies of Indians who had fallen to their death or leaped willingly. It was not until he had climbed to the camp itself that he entered the last circle of hell, a thousand corpses in every posture of repose covered by a live blanket of carrion eaters.

The Jesuit sank to his knees, clasping his Bible in his hands in prayer. "Hail Mary, Mother of God, pray for us sinners."

A vulture flopped in front of him, but the priest hit out. The bird ambled awkwardly toward the body of a boy, looked him over, then gave a tentative bite. The boy cried out with pain. For the second time in a day, Father Mercure's heart stopped still.

The child's ribs stuck out and he was filthy with the excrement of the birds. The Jesuit cried with happiness as he carried the small form over his shoulder to the river below. There was no doubt about it. The boy drank the water avidly and vomited and drank again and cried along with the priest. He was definitely alive. Father Mercure built a lean-to up stream and left the boy in it while he went back to search for other survivors. There were none. Even so, the Jesuit was filled with gratitude that he had been chosen to make the journey for the one life and he hummed as he walked away from the village a last time.

The boy was well and growing again when he and Father Mercure returned together to the Great Lakes. Nameless because he was not old enough to have had his vision, he became known as Christopher in the records of the Jesuit mission. Alert, aggressive, he was Father Mercure's best and favorite pupil. By the time he was fifteen, he was serving as the priest's personal secretary, transcribing discussions in French, English, and a number of Indian languages.

During the struggle between France and Italy for control of the papacy, Father Mercure was recalled to Europe and Christopher went with him. Special dispensation was obtained for the two to remain together when the Jesuit rose to a position in the Vatican diplomatic corps, Brother Christopher, as he was called, gaining an intimate education in the brokerage of politics. It was also a perfect viewpoint for the convulsions of 1848 when monarchy met socialism across the continent and won.

In 1851 Mercure and his secretary were dispatched to the Diocese of New York. It was there he discovered that the greatest revolutionary of his time, Garibaldi, was also in New York. Setter regarded him as "one of the few men alive capable of reshaping the future of Europe and the only man capable of unifying Italy into one nation." Setter managed to meet his hero, and during their brief but intense friendship, admitted that he hoped to write a book that would seize the conscience of his country.

Garibaldi scoffed at the idea of a "library victory," and so filled Setter's head with the necessity of learning how to win revolutions by actually taking part in one, that within a matter of days Setter boarded a three-master bound for Montevideo.

Here the biography of Where The Sun Goes becomes spotty. The most definite thing anyone can say is that he spent ten years in South America moving from one country and one revolution to another, almost as often as the seasons. His career in South America was in many ways similar to his mentor, Garibaldi's. He joined a freelance group of soldiers composed of native patriots, European idealists, and criminals from every part of the world. At first he was a messenger, then soldier, captain, and leader of his own band. Like Garibaldi, he took a wife who could fight with him and they had children. He never won any war, but he was not shot and killed. That in itself was a triumph.

John Setter emerged in London shortly after the American Civil War began. He was an importer with a fascinating supply of silver and gold artifacts from the New World; he never seemed to run out. Popular, and now unmarried, he was in demand at salons where Disraeli would read chapters from his novelettes. This was the fourth lifetime for Where the Sun Goes and it was the shortest. Having made his fortune, he left the door open to his shop one day and stepped onto the wharfs of New York a month later. He was just in time to read of the attempt to impeach President Johnson.

Soon he moved to Washington. Everyone else was going there to buy railroad land, sell timber, lease mines, or wallow through the public treasury on some other pretext. Setter seemed to be a different sort, quiet, reclusive, with a fanatical interest in history. He spent weeks in the libraries delving into the history of each Indian tribe, its religious beliefs, and its relations to white civilization. Often he would spend afternoons arguing with Lewis Henry Morgan, a railroad lobbyist from Rochester whose hobby was studying the Iroquois. Together, they went to the Smithsonian to see the brain of Mangus Colorado float in a jar of alcohol. Mangus Colorado was the Apache chief who had been assassinated by the army in Arizona during the war. A card in front of the jar said that the brain was heavier than Daniel Webster's.

Then John Setter disappeared from Washington, and during the nine years previous to the Greasy Grass it is said he traveled from one Indian nation to another, talking and listening, no matter whether the nation was forty thousand strong like the Lakota or were like the remains of the brave Wappo of California, only one hundred eighty left alive. "I did not promulgate insurrection. If this had proved necessary, I don't know what I would have done. Returned to Europe, turned to science or the solace of making money, all were possible if I had found my people as yet unready to take their last chance at liberty. Instead, affairs were at the point I had anticipated and all that was missing was the manager, a role I had groomed for all my life."

Setter's memoirs are overly modest. He did preach rebellion every chance he got, as attested to frequently in the Works of Wovoka and recorded conversations with They Fear His Horses. When he was not busy in this endeavor, he was preparing related operations in Canada and Europe. To some his will always be the work of the devil, to others the labor of a patriot. "It is a fictional nicety to present the centuries-old struggle of a people as the biography of one man," Setter wrote, declining to give the details of what that work or labor entailed.

General Nelson A. Miles was not so averse. "Some rascal's been riling the Indians and it's our job to stop the Indians and fix the rascal," he told his troops as they moved out to join MacKenzie's survivors at Fort Laramie. General Miles was known as a tough man who commanded at the front of his charge. His horse was a beautiful black thoroughbred that stepped lightly over the inch-thick snow covering the ground.

"I equipped my men as if they were going into Arctic regions," Miles wrote. This meant that to escape the numbing cold, the soldiers were dressing more and more like the Indians they were fighting. Shoddy greatcoats from shoddy manufacturers were burned for heat as the soldiers copied the bearskin coat made fashionable by their commander, a veteran of Plains warfare. Beaver gloves brought high prices. At night soldier and Indian curled up in buffalo robes that kept a man warm at minus thirty degrees. As the horse soldiers rode from Fort Keogh to Laramie, they put their bread between their stomachs and their coats to keep it from freezing.

A review was held outside Laramie for purposes of morale.

Speakers agreed that the reasons for revenge were multiplying and were, no doubt, foremost in the minds of the soldiers assembled. The official title of their next action was "Search and Destroy"; they were told and reassured that their nation knew they would do both. MacKenzie exhibited a new nervous tic.

Some people had doubts. Usually, winter meant the enlistment of hundreds of men throughout the frontier. They were known as "Snowbirds." Adventurers and bums, they joined for hot food during the bitter season and deserted with the first sign of spring. There were no Snowbirds this year, not one.

As the Snowbirds were conspicuous by their absence, the newspaper reporters were conspicuous for their great numbers. One correspondent had fallen with Custer. He was claimed by the *New York Herald Tribune* but he was actually from a Bismarck, North Dakota paper. "By the time this reaches you, we will have met and fought the red devils, with what results remains to be seen. I go with Custer and will be at the death," that unfortunate wrote. Now others clamored for his place, urged on by enormous bonuses offered by editors of every paper of decent circulation in the United States. The Indian War was proving the hottest item since Appomattox. Miles had them draw lots for the ten lucky men who would ride with him and MacKenzie.

He would have taken none if he hadn't received orders to assist in calming a jittery, curious public. There had been an election. General Rutherford B. Hayes was the new president on the force of a voting fraud in a pair of Southern states. People demanded confidence in their government and Hayes felt that reading about some military victories would do the trick. "Nellie," he wrote his old friend, "let the newsboys sit on the back of your horse just a little while." Commander of the armies, General Sherman, had returned to Washington with the election, and he wrote, "Bring back that scalp!"

Miles went hunting in the Valley of the Big Dry. He had practically no scouts left but his was a corps of professionals and contact with the enemy was soon made. Through the snow that continued to accumulate—it was now to their knees—the two grand forces maneuvered for position. The soldiers' camp was ringed every night by the steady glow of flares which stopped the grenade attacks, but which also helped the Indian marksmen who sniped away with their Kentucky long rifles at five hundred yards. General Miles was willing to accept the small losses so long as he felt he was driving the Indians to where the valley became a cul-de-sac.

"He must be running out of food, he must be running out of bullets, and I know damn well he's running out of room," Miles said in his dispatch to the Far West, the steamship headquarters.

A message came to Miles and MacKenzie, not from the Far West but from Sitting Bull by means of a lone warrior riding up to the advancing columns. "General: I want to know what you are doing traveling on this road. You scare all the buffalo away. I want to hunt in this place. If you turn back now, I will not fight you. Leave everything you have, all your rations and guns, and I will let you pass. You must let me know right now that you will do so. Your friend, Sitting Bull."

Since it was an offer no general would accept, the effort must be considered part of the Indian policy of recasting the Wasichu as strangers from another land without authority. Miles, for his answer, had a piece of wet rawhide tied around the messenger's throat, his hands tied to the pommel of his saddle. The Indian set off at a good pace to Sitting Bull but he was too late. The tightening leather cut off his wind just as he came into camp. The general and the chief knew where each other stood.

On the first day of December, Miles set up his forces in front of the triangular dead end of the Big Dry. His eight hundred foot soldiers were equally divided to close the flanks, making the triangle a funnel that would spill the Indians into his seven hundred infantry. Two batteries of howitzers sat behind the foot soldiers. At the end of the day, the army had bagged twenty deer and one bear. Miles reread his orders from Washington and sent back the report of a victory that had reestablished American sovereignty in the north. He did not list the number killed. The long-suffering reporters were told that the Indians had fled to Canada to escape the show by force.

MacKenzie went for his catch, an Indian force under the command of the Tsitsistas Yellow Nose in a canyon of Crazy Woman Fork along the Powder River. He was taking no chances this time. Captain Lawton of the Fourth Cavalry, his field quartermaster, was sent ahead to prepare stream crossings and bridges over ravines so that when cavalry and artillery moved it would be in one swift blow. Modern logistics would undo the Natives' cunning.

The same day of Miles's attack, MacKenzie and 1,110 horse soldiers, largely of the Fourth and Fifth Cavalry, and three mounted cannon raced down the Powder River Valley. Lawton's work was well done; the force covered in a morning what usually would have taken two days of slow going. With a definite target and a road to it, esprit ran high among the galloping troops. No one noticed a recurring phantom, the black sky rising behind them.

By the time they reached Yellow Nose's camp there was no mistaking the chill wind at their back. MacKenzie frenetically gave the battle orders in a race with the weather. If the snow fell before his attack was under way, the Indians would probably disappear in it and the hunt would have to start all over again. He would lead the first charge himself without benefit of the howitzer's softening shells. Lieutenant McKinney was in command of the other wing. Doing without bugles, the two lines formed a semicircle around the peaceful camp.

"They are about to come," Dull Knife said as he watched through field glasses. The other war chiefs stood beside him in a copse of trees above the camp. Tall Bull, Walking Whirlwind, Burns Red, and Hawks Visit listened to a description of the troops. "I think the big one will be first. He seems in a hurry. He doesn't have time to see that there are no women or babies in the camp."

Down in the camp two old men were being escorted through a ravine away from the action. Each carried a bundle decorated with eagle feathers and colored quills, one made of coyote fur and the other of buffalo. Whatever happened in the battle, neither could be jeopardized. The coyote fur covered the four sacred arrows, the buffalo fur the bison cap, the heart and soul of the Tsitsistas nation. If either were captured, no Cheyenne would fight again, for his power would be gone.

"Shallow, sir, no more than six inches from the looks of the water. No trouble," Lawton said.

MacKenzie glanced once over his shoulder at the dark sky and unsheathed his sword. The double line of horses moved forward first in a trot, then a canter, and by the time they reached the river, a full gallop. The blasts of the bugler were snatched away by the wind. The first soldier posted unnaturally and slid into the water, the front of his blue uniform a muddy maroon.

MacKenzie led a grand charge. The cavalry reached the camp at the height of its speed, giving the sharpshooters positioned in the first tipis little time to aim. Some of the defenders reverted to the old style of individual fighting and left their positions to die gloriously and fruitlessly. Dull Knife and Yellow Nose sent Four Spirits into the breastworks hidden among the tipis to maintain order. The mixed ranks of

Tsitsistas, Lakota, Arikara, and Inuna-ina fell back under the hooves of the attack, retreating from one line of defense to a second and a third. About fifty on each side fell during the first charge, with MacKenzie, wheeling on his horse and emptying his Colt, responsible for five of the enemy. A bugle sounded the second charge.

MacKenzie led his men to the side as McKinney's men dashed across the Powder. There was no doubt now that the Indians were falling back into the canyon walls behind the camp. The lieutenant and the Fourth and Fifth Cavalries went after them, racing straight through the smoldering camp and up the slopes. At first, MacKenzie could not believe his ears. The hills exploded in the rattle of the Gorloffs. McKinney dove from his horse, a dead man, and dozens more followed. In a matter of minutes there was just a rolling pile of men and mounts and no second charge.

"It's the Gatlings," MacKenzie yelled. He waved his arm to bring the troops back over the river. Once he had his howitzers rolled up, he would blast the machine guns off the walls. His men were headed back over the water when they saw the cannon already rolled forward with a squad of Indians led by Two Moons aiming the muzzles in their faces. The blizzard hid the death throes of MacKenzie's last command.

Riding with Miles was becoming popular with the correspondents. It was more like a triumphal procession with an enemy that would rather run than fight. All the same, this did not take away the romance of issuing dispatches headed "With Miles in Indian Country." They were learning how to ride and it was fun dressing up in buffalo coats and boots. No word had been received from MacKenzie and it was assumed by all that he was having as fine a time as they were.

Miles was moving down the Tongue River at a leisurely pace

looking for They Fear His Horses. Christmas and New Year were celebrated en route with double helpings of pork and the mysterious appearance of some whiskey. On January 8 the army was camped in a plateau surrounded by the Wolf Mountains, low lying humps with bare trees etched against the snow. An atmosphere of camaraderie suffused the tents as the general and a few of the reporters strolled by the wagons. The dusk turned to a pitch-black night pierced by diamond stars.

A pair of stars seemed to flash on the crest of a mountain.

"Comet?" suggested a reporter.

"Muzzle flashes," Miles said with no trace of doubt. Then they heard the distant report of guns and the explosion of a shell in the middle of the relaxing soldiers.

"The Indians have cannons?" the man from the *World* asked with a drooping jaw.

Miles didn't answer. He was running through the snow to his command tent as more shells came tearing into the camp. He saw more flashes from the mountains on the other side of the camp. A horse flew into the air ten feet away, rider and all. In back, a shell spun into the ammunition wagon the correspondents were huddled under.

The staff officers were waiting at the tent, suddenly sober with fear. "Major, you know where those guns are? You got their bearings? Then you take a hundred men, split them up and take those batteries. Don't take any more. If it's an ambush, that's all I want to lose," Miles said.

He ordered all campfires out and the wagons moved to new locations over the shattered planks of those that couldn't be moved. The horses were shifted around those that couldn't walk. The plateau became as dark as a sea. The howitzers stopped firing, but the major and his hundred men did not return.

Dawn was a frigid, grey affair. The soldiers' buffalo robes

were encrusted with ice. Light revealed the wounds left by thirty odd shells that had fallen in the night.

Dawn also brought more shells from a solid ring of cannon around the camp. Miles nodded in his field chair, his coat drawn up to his nose. "Uh-huh, uh-huh. Sucked us in. Thought they'd start up again." Plumes of smoke erupted from the snow. There was no sun, only a lighter grey. The staff officers stood around the chair like sleepless acolytes. The men on their stomachs across the field kept their eyes on the tent.

"Sir, don't you think we should start digging trenches?" a captain said.

"Waste of breath on a bitter day like today," Miles said. "Got us boxed in and nailed down, boys, give them credit. Give them credit but don't help them out. That trench'd be your grave. What's the nearest fort?"

"Laramie, sir."

Miles ordered his two cannons sighted on the smoke of the Indian guns firing from a southern ridge. Major Casey was given the honor of clearing the ridge for the rest of the force. The army drew itself together as Casey's two companies rode off. Miles mounted his black thoroughbred in open view, ignoring the shell bursts. When he saw the Indian guns on the ridge cease firing under the reply from his own batteries and Casey halfway up the hill, he gave the order to move out.

It was a wise and lucky plan. To stay would have been disastrous, and the hill they chose to break through was one of the few without Gorloffs. Miles was able to bring his force through the trees as a unit and head home. Quickly a number of disadvantages made themselves obvious to him. The Indians could move much faster than the soldiers because they were nearly one hundred percent cavalry. If the troopers stopped for a rest, the Indians were able to begin shelling again. He had no idea of how many they were, while they knew exactly how many he had. These problems had never risen before because the Indians never stayed together in the winter before and they had never had cannon before. Miles ran his hands through his silver hair. The Indians had not been drawn into a set piece battle yet; that was something else to consider.

Noon found the soldiers on a butte. The retreat had stopped. Infantry and cavalry were deployed by squads, platoons, companies, battalions, and regiments in lines and rectangles and boxes. Inside were the wagons, the ambulances, and Miles. The United States Army waited for a fight. They waited the whole day. Nothing touched the snow around them but the wind.

"What kind of an enemy is this?" Miles asked himself. As the soldiers pitched camp, the first shells began arriving.

Sitting Bull, They Fear His Horses, and Big Crow rode by the cannon as the dawn of the second day approached. They looked not toward the stricken camp but to the west. A rider was pushing toward them relentlessly over the ice, waving his arms in excitement long before he reached the campfire. Warriors along the route who recognized what his message was shouted with glee. They Fear His Horses slapped Big Crow on the shoulder.

"They are only a few miles away. I have seen them," the rider said as his winded pony halted in front of the chiefs.

An hour later they appeared, a host from the west. Nimipu, Northern Shoshone, Western Shoshone, Kalispel, and Skitswish, nine thousand in all, following Thunder Going Over The Mountains, the man called Chief Joseph by the Wasichu. He had led them almost two thousand miles, over three armies. First there was General Howard and the First Cavalry on the Lolo Trail, then General Gibbon in the Bitterroot Mountains, and finally Colonel Sturgis at Canyon Creek. Thunder Going Over The Mountains had beaten them all, picking up other nations as he came. With the warriors he had, the force facing General Miles totaled twenty-five thousand men.

From Idaho Territory, telegraph operators were furiously trying to send a message to General Miles telling him of the death and wounding of Howard and Gibbon and the coming of the Nez Percé. The effort got no further than the first uprooted telegraph pole.

Far to the south similar messages were being sent over the desert by heliographs. There were twenty-seven of the reflecting mirrors posted on mesa tops and they could send flashes in Morse code for fifty miles at a leap. This day they told General Ben Grierson that the Ninth Cavalry had been beaten back into Fort Bayard.

"Was there anything else, any guess when they might get out?" Grierson asked the rider.

"Nope. I waited for a couple of hours at the station but nothing else came. Like it went dead."

"Thanks. Find yourself some food." Grierson walked across the dusty floor of the mission house buckling his belt. A stomach wound had fouled up his digestive system and he grimaced at the sight of a plate of tacos on a table.

A wagon was being turned over at the entrance of the adobe wall. His soldiers, most from the Tenth Cavalry, found what shade they could to rest in. A Gatling on top of the house and two prewar cannons made up the heavy arms. He had stood off the Apache in Taos for two weeks so far. That wasn't bad.

Help was supposed to come from Bayard or Fort Quitman. The trouble was that every rescue party that emerged vanished in a canyon, apparently as easily as the heliograph messages. Grierson had figured it out but it was too late and he knew it. They were supposed to just be fighting Apache. The trouble was that Grierson was fighting Apache while the other commanders were fighting Comanche and Caddo and Kiowa, each regiment up against a whole tribe. It didn't make sense, knowing Indians, but he got some humor out of being proved right over his dead body.

His son, just returned from an Eastern college, called in from the door. "There's another delegation coming, Dad. Get ready."

Grierson checked his buttons and put on his hat. He disguised a burp as a yawn as the delegation marched in.

"General, this has gone far enough. We demand your protection as citizens of the United States," the first one said. They were all alike, red-faced farmers gripping rifles like hoes.

Grierson shrugged.

"Gentlemen, what can I say? I invited you here to this mission so that I could protect you. Instead, you change your minds and take your families to a rancho I can hardly see from here. I can't protect you if you refuse to stay and, as I've told you a number of times, this is the best place to defend. Together we might stand a chance. Separated like this for no good reason, we'll just watch each other die."

"It's a very good reason," a squat shotgun toter said. "You know the reason. And you know that it's your duty to protect white folks."

"You have a hundred rifles," Grierson persisted. "Add them to my soldiers and who knows? Maybe we'll get out of this mess. It's not easy to forget old customs, but we're talking about survival now . . ."

"We didn't come West to fight alongside no Negroes," the shotgun said.

"It's a fact that the Tenth Cavalry is a Negro outfit," Grierson said. "Probably the finest soldiers out here. I'm sure Victorio and Geronimo think so. To deny their help is a sin."

"Don't tell us about sin," a farmer said with a shudder as he shot a glance at the blacks along the wall.

"You won't come or send your officers over?" the squat one asked.

"That's right."

"Then we demand that you turn over your machine gun and your cannon. That's the least you can do for your own kind."

Grierson looked them over. They had absolute belief in what they were saying, so much so that he felt odd man out. Most of the new settlers were from the South, a new South with the old ideals. Maybe in some strange way it was his duty to go with them, guns and all.

"Thank you, gentlemen. I think I know my own kind."

A weird sort of comprehension seemed to come over their faces. Grierson had never seen anything so obscene in his life. "Oh. Yeah. Yeah. Now we get it," they muttered among themselves.

"Get out," Grierson said. "My invitation, the invitation of my men, is withdrawn."

A shotgun barrel was shoved into his stomach. "That's what we thought you'd say, General. So we're telling you. Give us the Gatling and the cannon or I'll blast your guts all over this room." In agreement, all of the rifles rested on Grierson's chest.

It was a clean-cut situation more to the general's liking. To the delegation's dismay, he relaxed.

"If you so much as touch me," he said with a grim smile, "those black bucks out there will kill every last mother's son of you. That's not going to help your families much. Because for all I know, these jigs are going to greet the Apache like lost brothers and they're all going over to the rancho to torture your wives and rape your daughters."

The farmers were shaking with pure hate but the guns turned back into hoes. They left without a word to him or his soldiers.

Grierson rubbed his belly and went outside, checking with

the officers along the waist-high wall. Soldiers laid strips of gunpowder on the ground beyond. His son tied ropes to ammunition bags so that they could be dragged by men under fire. In the kiva turned hospital, the wounded who couldn't hold a gun sweated in polite misery. Half of Grierson's six hundred men were casualties, most from the ambush that drove him and the Tenth Cavalry into the small New Mexican pueblo. None of this explained the strange cheerfulness with which he faced the inevitable. As he mounted the outside stairs to the Gatling, he wondered if this was the sensation that George Custer had had.

The clearinghouse for news from the frontier was St. Louis. Sherman was in Washington with his title and his friends and General Phil Sheridan, the Union bantam cock, was in charge of military activity west of Fort Leavenworth. The first order he sent out to all forts was:

"Disarm all Indians on reservations. Kill all Indians off reservations."

New camps were readied for captured Indians at Fort Marion, Florida, to supplement the ones already full. President Hayes went before Congress with a promise to make secure the future of every homesteader and read to the representatives a letter sent to him by a group of Christian Indians asking for protection against non-Christian Indians.

The trouble was that what was left of the United States Army between California and Kansas was holed up behind the wooden palisades of their forts. It was February before the full impact of what had happened hit the East. That was when the settlers, untouched by the Indians, swarmed back over the Missouri with their possessions on their backs, surrounding Kansas City, St. Louis, and San Antonio with great tent cities. Despite the government's efforts, the papers rooted out the tales of the ghost regiments. New names joined Custer's in the public memory.

Crook's Retreat. The Tongue River Massacre. Grierson's Last Stand. And when Goy-ya-thle had fulfilled his fantasy, they said, "Remember Tucson!"

"It is a standing disgrace to us, that a nation of forty million civilized, and to a great extent, Christian people, is utterly unable to deal in any credible manner with a few thousands of so-called savages within easy reach," wrote the Reverend Edward Jacker in an article entitled "Who Is to Blame for the Indian Disaster?" in the *American Quarterly Catholic Review*. The author suggested that the great misfortune of the Sioux Nation was that it had never accepted Jesuit missionaries.

The *New York Herald*'s front page editorial called for the elimination of the Indian problem on a permanent basis. Others talked of the "Texas Solution," by which the settlers of that state had wiped out the native inhabitants. The Texas Rangers were created for that sole purpose. In California it was known as "Ben Wright's Way" after a local Indian agent who'd invited forty of his charges to a feast and slaughtered them with a Gatling for bounty. Still, the settlers, a hundred thousand of them, poured out of the Indian Territory and, as soon as they were safe, formed vigilante committees. The House and Senate voted unanimously for an increase in the size of the army to seventy-five thousand. The creation of a settlers' militia twice the size of the army was also authorized.

By the end of February, the United States struck back. A mob of displaced homesteaders wiped out the last traces of the Huron Nation, two hundred fifty women and children, on its Oklahoma reservation.

"I want to be seen. I want people to see that an Indian is a human," Holds Eagles said. He turned the convertible down Connecticut Avenue. "Besides, it's a nice day for a drive."

Liz Carney looked around at the people on the street. They

were staring at the dark man in a fine buckskin shirt with swirling beads behind the wheel of the car.

"It's just a bad day for this," Liz said. "Right after VV Day. Feelings are running pretty high."

"People are less inclined to kill other people," he said, "but once they can convince themselves their enemy isn't human, anything goes. That's a loose translation from Moose Who Saw A Moon. Simple thought and a true one."

"If you mean you'd like to prove you're mortal, you may end up doing that. What about those agents you were hinting about a couple of days ago, the ones who tried to stop you?"

Holds Eagles raised an eyebrow.

"Did I say that?" He slowed down to read a sign. "It's been a long time since I was in Washington. How do we get to some country?"

"Take a plane. There is still some open ground around a few of the more expensive co-op apartments. That's why we want some of your land, remember?"

Holds Eagles snapped a finger. "That's right."

"You think we can share this continent?" she said, slipping back to her role as a reporter.

"We do now."

A car pulled alongside, traveling at the same speed. It was a family, mother and father in front and the kids in back still hanging on to their ragged VV Day banners. A boy saw Holds Eagles through the window and the eyelids drew back from his eyeballs. He shouted and his father turned to hit him, but then he saw Holds Eagles. The car swerved into another lane and back. The mother exercised new muscles as her nose pulled itself up with disgust. Her eyes bored into Liz Carney. Her husband shoved an arm past her and a meaty middle finger sprang up. The boy used the stick of the banner as an imaginary machine gun and riddled the convertible. His little sister tried to join in by smiling and waving.

"Well, you have been seen and bitten the dust," Liz said. A helicopter fluttered far overhead, making a copy of the convertible's path.

"Why should we believe you?" President Nielson asked the next day.

Holds Eagles waited for the president to finish what he had to say. It was something that he learned right away; that the president wanted to deal in specifics but had trouble doing so. Peripherally he took in the Georgian-Hawaiian atmosphere of the negotiating room, the president's advisers seated down one side of the long table with Holds Eagles and Bearman alone on the other side.

"Do you know what I mean?" Nielson asked, as if Holds Eagles were supposed to say he understood how distrustful Indians were. "What you people did during the war was not commendable. Your lack of support while we were making this part of the world safe in Vietnam was . . . sad. I regret the incident leading to Buffalo Rider's death, but that's the sort of thing you have to expect when you allow controversy to grow."

The president babbled on to the agreeing nods of his advisers. Holds Eagles diverted his mind to other matters. Such as how a democratic process could continually spew forth men of Nielson's caliber. He thought of the Lenape Buffalo Rider, so happy to be a man of peace after a lifetime as a warrior. The trip to the border when the United States made its first demand. The speeches by Buffalo Rider and the American secretary of state, a man who honestly desired peace. The man in the black windbreaker who somehow walked through the police lines and shot Buffalo Rider and the secretary each three times in the head and chest before being wrestled to the ground. Dog Soldiers had been asked by Buffalo Rider to let the Wasichu handle the security as a gesture of trust.

". . . Indeed, there has even been some doubt expressed as to your ability to communicate with your superiors."

It was his turn to speak, Holds Eagles realized. He ignored what the president had said.

"The Indian Nation understands your concern over problems of overpopulation and of communication between the two halves of your great nation. We would like to do what we can to help a neighbor. One of these ways, we believe, would be to allow commercial air paths over the Indian Nation between the Western and Eastern United States. At the same time, the Indian Nation would expect reciprocation in terms of air terminals for the Indian airline. Cables could be laid across the continent that both our countries might use. In terms of overpopulation, Indian experts stand ready to aid the United States in preparing land in the vast reaches of Alaska for your people. It is not impossible that other mutual solutions might develop from these talks.

"At the same time, I would like to add that I agree that controversies such as the one we are faced with, and will overcome, draw forth extremists. Like yourself, I deplore extremism in any form. With you, I would say to the extremists on either side that the mutual borders of the United States and the Indian Nation have stood unchanged for almost one hundred years. It is almost impossible to find on earth borders made more sacrosanct by the passage of time. Wars and distrust have erased lines everywhere else; here mutual respect has made our border all the more solid. Neither you nor I would give in to extremists no matter what the pressure. The cause of peace is too important and the cost of war too terrible."

"Goddamn snake in the grass didn't hear a word I said. Thing was a goddamn waltz," President Nielson said later in his breakfast room. It was evening but the president and his staff needed some place they could eat and analyze the opening statements at the same time. Everyone was in shirtsleeves, surrounded by underlined sheets of paper and crustless sandwiches. "Waltz."

"Wants to help us settle a glacier," a staffer said with admiration.

"I didn't know about the age of our borders with the Indians," Vice President Ho said.

"They've never been officially recognized," the attorney general said. "We didn't agree to them until 1918 and we didn't officially recognize them. I suppose you spotted that threat in 'the cost of war too terrible,'" he asked the president.

"Yes, and the way he twisted things about extremists. There aren't any Indians trying to take land away from us, are there?"

"They wouldn't dare," Moore said.

Chapter Four

> He yoho! He yoho ho!
> The yellow-hide, the white-skin.
> I have now put him aside—
> I have now put him aside—
> I have no more sympathy with him,
> I have no more sympathy with him.
> He yoho ho! He yoho ho!
>
> —God, in Inuna-Ina song

The population of the United States in 1877 was forty million people. One hundred thousand Indians had swept the United States Army, what was left of it, from the field. "It was the year that made the impossible possible," claimed an amateur historian at the time. "The country was in a deep malaise. Sick with the strain of the Civil War, sick with cynicism of the Railroad Age, sick with a surfeit of immigrants unable to speak the English language, it didn't have the spirit to combat the fanaticism of the Red Man."

Theodore Roosevelt's theory was the popular one of the

nineteenth century, the wrong one. John Setter's theory, the one the Indians used, was simpler. The United States, the great new industrial cyclops, was sick with its own greed. It was a giant sunk to its waist in a swamp of greed, powerful and impotent at the same time.

The railroads and the barons who ran them tried to take over the last third of the continent in one enormous bite. They thought they could do it and they persuaded the rest of the Americans that they could. As the tracks ran west, a nation got on board, speculating on silver, gold, land, timber, wheat, corn; on cattle, pigs, sheep; on copper, cotton, iron; on anything, anything at all. After an arduous struggle, the people saw themselves gaining a paradise that was their birthright and the reward of laissez-faire capitalism.

"By God, it's a great century!" Jay Gould said on the floor of the New York Stock Exchange in 1870.

In 1877 things were different. Jay Gould, idol of the masses, was stopped on the street by a man who pushed him into a doorway and beat him to a pulp. Bystanders stood around and laughed. A policeman kept order among the spectators but he was laughing too. The man dusted off his hands and walked away to cheers. Gould did not bother to press charges. He had already been beaten in the same manner by other men twice that year. The romance and the promises of the railroad development schemes had worn thin in seven years. Since the start of the Depression in 1873, most of the grand names behind the iron roads were accompanied by bodyguards.

Expansion had stopped in the west as vast land developments fell through. Gould's railroad, like most of the others, was in the hands of creditors. People who had invested in the railroads read about the bribery of the vice president, about the credit mobilier scandal, about the congressional scandals, about the government loan scandals, about scandals that came on top of each other day after day between layers of denials after denials. They were confused but they knew one thing. Men like Gould spent the afternoon buying a diamond while they spent the afternoon looking for a job.

Everyone, except for a sonorous few, the unshakable captains of industry, seemed to be looking for a job. One out of four men in the United States had no job at all while the rest looked for something that would pay better than ten cents an hour. When night came to New York City, eighty thousand homeless people came in to police stations to keep warm until the next day. It meant that one tenth of the nation's greatest city lived in prison, voluntarily or involuntarily.

There had never been anything like the Depression. Thrift, strength, intelligence, perseverance meant nothing as whole towns shut down. People understood droughts or plagues or natural disasters, but to the unsophisticated worker of that era the normal exhale of industry was a new mystery, like an epidemic without a disease. In their frustration, hiding in shanty towns, they heard how the Homestead Act was used by big companies to seize land on the frontier. A thousand acres of fertile ground was staked out by company agents, leaving nothing but scrub for the family farmer.

Reform was dead, murdered in the ultimate of scandals in a scandal-staggered time. Samuel Tilden, the most famous fighter of corruption in the country, was elected president by a quarter of a million votes on November 7, 1876. In electoral votes he won 196 to 173 over General Rutherford Hayes, the Republican candidate. Then the spoils machine went to work. In Florida, a mass shipment of cash wrapped in threats went to the vote returning boards and the votes of Democratic precincts were disallowed. The chairman of the board admitted all later when a promised appointment didn't come through, but by then it was too late. Florida had four electoral votes. The same combination worked in Louisiana on November 8. Louisiana had eight electoral votes. Tilden still had a quarter million votes more, but the switches made Hayes president, 185 electoral votes to 184. With little finesse and in broad daylight, the presidency of the United States was stolen.

There was some talk about a rebellion to save the nation's honor. The publisher of the Louisville *Courier-Journal*, a Republican, printed a call for a hundred thousand men to defend the capital. Rumors spread about the camps of soldiers in Washington waiting for such a popular protest but talk of rebellion soon ended.

There were other things to talk about, President Hayes and the newspapers and the Republicans said, mainly the insult of the Indian uprising. *The Herald*, the *Cincinnati Commercial*, the *Chicago Tribune* and others promised to outfit lads willing to try their fortune against the wiles of the savage. Circulation rose rapidly along with the private armies. Businessmen saw what war was doing for the papers and in the back of their minds a faint bell rang, reminding them of the good times when Grant was going through a thousand uniforms a day. President Hayes didn't need any prompting to say what he would do.

The president's "Call to Red Americans" was printed in the newspapers on March 13 alongside laudatory editorials. He denounced the "unfair voices that claim the only good Indian is a dead Indian." He was replying to these voices, Hayes said, by making all Indians full citizens of the United States with all Constitutional rights. This meant, of course, that all treaties were null and void as the government could not have treaties with its citizens. Treaty land would be open to the public under the Homestead Act. In return for this act of executive recognition,

Hayes demanded one act of faith to the government: service in the Army on the frontier for all Indian males between the ages of twenty and forty. "Through their own efforts, they are thus offered an opportunity to end the vilification of their race," he concluded. It was generally agreed that Hayes had pulled a tactical coup, accomplishing in one generous measure what others had failed to do since the colonies began, separating the Indians from their land.

The following day there was a smaller item in the papers. The Department of War announced that actions on the frontier had cost approximately twenty million dollars so far, not including loss to property, and that estimated expenditures to the successful end of the fighting were fifty million dollars. New taxes were asked.

The headlines were reserved for General Sheridan as he massed his army on the fields surrounding Fort Leavenworth. Raw recruits were being whipped into shape by gruff sergeants. An infantry as large as the Sioux Nation itself was marching over the grass. Twenty thousand fresh cavalry raced through maneuvers. Veterans of the War Between the States enlisted with their sons and with their old adversaries. Five-foot-four Phil Sheridan was photographed with Buffalo Bill, who was going to slaughter as many of the buffalo as he could in an effort to eliminate the Red Man's source of nutrition, the *Times* said. Sheridan was quoted as planning to use his "friendly Indians" as shock troops. "The main idea is to lose as few American soldiers as possible," he said. Immense troop trains were readied in St. Louis. Correspondents wandered through the tent towns of the settlers, searching for tales of Indian atrocities. There was no lack of stories even though there seemed to be no lack of settlers, either.

The country at large was settling back for some healthy diversion and outrage. In April right-thinking people were shocked to learn that no word had been received from Salt Lake City despite a dozen messengers. One or two papers printed the news with a black border of mourning. By April, too, people were beginning to ask when Sheridan's army would move out into the field. The War Department explained that plans to transport the troops by train had not anticipated the destruction of railroad beds by the Indians. Senators from Nebraska, Minnesota, Iowa, Kansas, Oklahoma, Nevada, California, Texas, and Oregon got on a train to see the general.

The meeting was held on May 1 in the command tent of the newly reformed Seventh Cavalry. Sheridan used a pointer as tall as himself to outline the task on a colored map. The senators quickly changed from critics to fascinated junior officers.

"The War Between the States was largely one of strategic centers, the way all wars are between civilized opponents. If you take the enemy's sources of industry, seize his means of transportation, and merely hold his armies to a tie, then you will win. It's as simple as that. We are fighting a different kind of enemy, though," Sheridan said.

"He has no industry to take. No fixed centers of population to hold. He and his ponies are his own means of transportation. In other words, there is only one way to defeat him. That is, to kill him. No cities or states will matter in this war; only bodies."

"That's where our Indians come in," the senior senator from Minnesota said.

"That's right. I realize that all of you from states that border the hostilities are anxious to know where your army is going to operate first. There's been a good deal of pressure to go into Colorado, especially since Colorado Territory would have become a state last year if it hadn't been for the outbreaks. I wouldn't call it political pressure, rather concern for the security of a new member of the Union." Sheridan turned his face to the map to hide the outright shock at his own words. Bill Sherman said war was hell, but politics was something else.

"As it happens," he went on, "Colorado is the natural field of action for us. Through it, we can join the Pacific states and at the same time sever the tribes. I'm sure the senators here from California, Nevada, and Oregon were wondering when we could provide them with troops. Well, there are two ways. Sending them by ship around the Cape or marching them right through the enemy. Second way's faster and accomplishes half the job on the way. So that's what we're going to do. I can't be more specific because when the enemy shows up we're going to chase him if he hides in the North Pole. But we'll get him. I feel that the Indians will be smashed within two years. Mopping up operations might go on for some time after that."

The senior senator from Kansas held his hands up with a tolerant grin. "Senators, I think we've imposed on General Sheridan long enough. He's been very patient and I think now that we're getting into areas that are his jurisdiction I feel confident that we have the right man for the job. I worried when I read the president's announcement about good Indians—whether this effort would be pressed with the necessary zeal. Now I remind myself that it was you, wasn't it, General, who said, 'The only good Indian is a dead Indian'?"

On the first day of July, the right man marched out of Leavenworth his army of forty thousand cavalry, fifty thousand infantry, thirty thousand Indian conscripts, three hundred fifty-five cannon, three hundred Gatling guns, twenty thousand wagons, fifteen thousand teamsters, and one hundred ambulances. The send-off was accompanied by the Army Symphony of the West. Great numbers of families had come from St. Louis and small towns throughout Kansas to enjoy the ceremonies and blessings. Conestogas open to the air carried young ladies prepared to wave handkerchiefs. Newspaper correspondents, not only from the East but from Europe, and photographers lugging their camera obscura machinery, all etched in their minds the leave-taking of the *Grande Armée*.

Sheridan was to strike through Colorado to Utah and then into Nevada, leaving a wake of new, fully manned forts. Scarves painted with the proposed route sold like hotcakes. William Almon Wheeler, vice president, addressed the crowd from the platform. Three people died from heat stroke. The band struck up "Garryowen." Like a huge, stippled snake, the army moved onto the prairie.

They were leaving a different nation behind. Something was new. For the first time in many years, there were almost no Indians in the eastern part or the western coastal areas known as the United States of America. Hayes had ended all that as states and mobs rushed to relieve the new citizens of their homes and introduce them into the army with foot chains. Old resentments were paid off. The League of the Longhouse, the Iroquois who were building their own empire when the English came, held large reservations in New York, Pennsylvania, even Oklahoma. For a long time people had disliked the arrogant League, which included the Seneca, Mohawk, Onondaga, Oneida, Cayuga, St. Regis, and Tuscarora. The Mohican went the same way, and the Catawba in South Carolina. The Powhatan in Virginia had helped Nat Turner; that debt was settled. The Nanticoke with its slave blood were locked into cattle cars. The Cherokee who had escaped the March of Tears to Oklahoma and returned to fight for the South escaped again, this time into the swamps with the Ikaniksalgi, that blend of hunted Creek, black, and Spanish that was called Seminole. North, the Iroquois were bribing their guards and slipping over the border to Canada.

Oklahoma means Red Man. Strangely, when the militia

came to round up the Indians in Oklahoma, there weren't many red men. All the same, they took what they could find from the reservations of the departed Ikaniksalgi and Cherokee and Iroquois, Muskogee, Chickasaw, Sawnee, Choctaw, Tuskegee, Quapaw, Hutanga, Wichita, and Caddo. It seems that the nations had heard what became of the Hurons. The militia ended up shooting to settle ranch claims.

Texas had a reputation for knowing how to deal with Indians. There were just a few miserable Alabama huts shivering on the border. It was expected that the Lone Star State would provide an army of its own to help in solving the problems next door in New Mexico, but people had forgotten that Texas's main concern was not Indians but Mexico, which still claimed Texas as its own. When a regiment of Mexican dragoons suddenly appeared along the Rio Grande, Texas decided to watch out for itself.

In California, Oregon, and Washington Territory, there were no roundups. There was hardly any need. Of every ten tribes that existed a hundred years before, only one existed now, and it was but a tenth its former size. There was little point in trying to form troops out of the tattered remains of the Pacific Indians. Vigilantes showed up at villages, shot those they found, and turned into prospectors.

Of the ones they didn't find, their remains were scattered through the hills east to Nevada and Arizona and Idaho where the Indians held sway. They came alone or in families or in groups of a hundred, but they came. Klallam, Sinkiuse, Skuyelpe, Klickitat, Lummi, Kwenetchetchat, Methow, Nisqually, Nooksack, Isonkuaili, Puyallup, Quileute, Quinault, Sahewamish, Sanpoil, Senijextee, Humaluh, Snohomish, Snoqualmie, Spokane, Suquamish, Tuadhu, Walla Walla, Winatca, Echeloot, and Pakintlema from Washington. Alsea, Atfalati, Kalapuya, Wailetpu, Shista-kwusta, Chetco, Guithlakimas, Hanis, Maklaks, Lohim,

Miluk, Modoc, Siletz, Melilema, Tututni, Tyigh, Etnamitane, Wasco, and Watlala from Oregon. Achomawi, Alliklik, Atsugewi, Kawia, Tantawats, Chimariko, Chumash, Kupa, Diegueño, Hupa, Karuk, Kato, Pomo, Kawaiisu, Miwok, Kitanemuk, Mattole, Koso, Lassik, Luiseño, Maidu, Cow-ang-a-chem, Shasta, Tolowa, Bahkanapul, Wailaki, Wappo, Whilkut, Wintun, Sulatelik, Yokuts, Yuki, Ukhotnom, and Yurok from California. They disappeared forever with their names, but together they added forty thousand to their brothers on the plains.

Sheridan didn't see any yet. The grassland looked bare all the way to the western coast. He took advantage of that fact to have his officers train his Indians. Contrary to the president's message, it seemed that the only Indians Sheridan had were on the wrong sides of twenty and forty. Men of fighting age had dematerialized, leaving boys barely able to hold a rifle and old men too senile to know the right end of one. It did not make for a heady pace, and after a week Sheridan's main body was barely seventy miles out of Leavenworth. He had junior officers pick out the most decrepit, crippled, or underage, march them out on the prairie, and lose them.

By the second week, Sheridan was two hundred miles out and right inside the skin of Indian controlled ground. He set his men to work building their first fortress. "Fighting Phil" was on his way.

On July 14, a Saturday, forty firemen and brakemen of the Baltimore Ohio Railroad walked off their jobs in Camden Station, Maryland. They quit because of a ten percent cut in their pay, the third ten percent cut in three years.

On Sunday more men walked off the job. By the end of the week, fifty thousand workers refused to go to work. So far as they were concerned, the Depression had gone far enough. They were getting off, and they weren't alone. Another fifty thousand men, not railroad workers, walked off their jobs in sympathy. They were peaceful but sincere. They had had enough. The owners of the railroads said that the strikers were Communists.

The first violence came within two days after the Camden Station walk out as B&O workers in Martinsburg, West Virginia, put down their tools to protest the cut. Governor Henry Matthews was telegraphed the news. He called out the state militia.

The state militia was not large and half of it refused to come because they agreed with the mob. Tuesday morning two companies of militia did arrive and met eight hundred people at the station. A train started out under military protection and someone tried to stop it. He shot a guardsman and the guardsman killed him. In seconds, everyone was shooting. The train crew ran and then the militia ran. At the request of Governor Matthews, President Hayes declared the state of West Virginia in insurrection.

Thursday, five companies of US infantry marched into Martinsburg and pushed the mob out of the station. Only two trains went west that day, though. There weren't any train crews to take more. The refusal to run the trains was the decision of the Brotherhood of Locomotive Engineers.

Martin Irons, head of the Knights of Labor, struck in the Southwest, tying up five thousand miles of track throughout Missouri, Arkansas, and Nebraska. The governors of the three states issued appeals that the strikers call off the slow down for patriotic reasons; military hardware was backing up on lines throughout the nation. Elected officials of the people were starting to realize that fervor for the war was not as deep as they had thought.

The railroad guilds thought they could control the anger of the jobless mobs. They could not. By Friday, six days after the strikes started, Pennsylvania's Governor Hartranft called out the state militia, just a few hours before Maryland's Governor Carroll sent militia to clear a mob from the Cumberland railroad junction. The explosive mixture of starvation, impotence, and anger had aged in its bottle long enough and nobody could find the cork.

Torches were blazing all across the nation. Baltimore was the scene of an extensive domestic battle between mobs of thousands of homeless and jobless sympathizers of the striking railroad men, and troops led by the commander of the Eastern United States, General Winfield Scott Hancock. The Pittsburgh, Pennsylvania, railroad yards were no longer the "Gateway to the West." There, mobs had taken over the entire city, looting Johnson's gun factory and the Company F armory. Federal troops, armed with Gatlings, had moved into the railroad yard's huge roundhouse. Railroad cars drenched in petroleum were sent down the tracks into the roundhouse until its walls were sheets of fire.

President Hayes convened a special cabinet meeting on Sunday, July 22. Riding high on the wave of military adventure a week before, the president was now in the depths of depression. At a time when the nation should have been falling shoulder to shoulder in the common effort of winning a war, it was tearing itself apart over the issue of wages.

"It's Communist agitators," everyone at the long table agreed. Hayes shook his head in fatigue.

"Our fault," he said. "The immigration policies have been lax, very lax. You don't preserve apples in a barrel by adding rotten ones. The question is what do we do about the ones we have?"

It was decided to have the police break up all Communist and Socialist meetings, to arrest and put in preventive detention all suspected Communist and Socialist leaders as subversive aliens. They were orders that the president could take pleasure in giving. The other orders broke his heart.

Pennsylvania, Maryland, and West Virginia were declared in a state of siege. Federal troops were also dispatched to Illinois in anticipation of an announcement of a state of siege.

A call for twenty thousand volunteers, the most that could be expected since the raising of Sheridan's army, was broadcast in newspapers.

And Sheridan's army was ordered to turn back.

In the face of Hayes's strong measures, the violence was expected to recede. Instead, it increased. From Buffalo to New Orleans, San Francisco to Philadelphia, the disenchanted citizens confronted the troops of their own government in the streets. The nation had gone through an earthquake. Hundreds were dead, millions of dollars of damage was done as cities almost burned to the ground. "Fighting Phil" Sheridan's picture was in the New York *Tribune* with the child's rhyme:

The noble Duke of York,
He had ten thousand men,
He marched them up to the top of the hill,
And he marched them down again.

Whatever the convulsions of the Depression violence did to the United States, like a patient saved by a miracle, the country was subtly changed. The clamor for war against the Indians suddenly struck it as not absolutely necessary for survival when it had barely survived itself. Even the avid propagandists were trying to catch their breath.

When Buffalo Bill appeared in New York in a personal appeal and Wild West show for the benefit of wounded Indian fighters, Nast cartooned him, complete with bandages, crutch, and money belt, as the head invalid.

"Having passed through the vale of anarchy and still trembling in exhaustion from the effort of merely keeping itself whole, the country at large should be permitted to ask whether it may learn something of value from its experiences," said Charles Francis Adams of Massachusetts in an interview with a Boston paper. He was an honest man, so haughty with virtue that the nation listened. "What it might discover is the reason for the national sympathy for the strikers, which is that the strikers were expressing a national distaste for the machinations of the railroads, a business marked for its scandalous conduct whether it be in our political or our business life. No other group of men has been so responsible for the sad state of our land economically or morally. Indeed, what has been the common factor in all these disputes? The railroads. Even the mines of Pennsylvania where immigrant workers revolted from slave labor are owned by the railroads. What we have just gone through, at a cost of life and incalculable loss of property, is a Railroad War. The question now is whether the American people care to take arms at another huge expenditure of lives and money against the native inhabitants of the Middle Desert for another Railroad War, for surely it is the railroads who will profit and not the families who will go without food so that guns may be bought."

The phrase "the Railroad War" attached itself to the frontier campaign like a magnet. Cartoons of Jay Gould and Jim Fisk as self-proclaimed homesteaders proliferated. Emerson wrote from Concord to his old anti-slavery friends that killing Americans as a diversion from the killing of Americans, the trade of frontier war for domestic war, was morally indefensible.

The Senate hearing of September 2, however, turned up a fiscal immorality. The lawmakers had at first gone along with the

War Department estimate of fifty million dollars for the rest of the war. Then the cities began burning. It was a crude method but it let the representatives of the people know that they were angry about wages and taxes and that they didn't like railroads.

General Sherman testified that a regiment cost one million dollars a year to maintain in active service, not including the cost of horses for cavalry, pay, or weaponry.

A senator did some rapid arithmetic. "According to my figures," he said, "that comes to about four hundred sixty-eight million dollars, not fifty million dollars, to send the new seventy-five thousand-man army into action."

The idea was to let Sherman explain the discrepancy away. The fifty million was based not on seventy-five thousand men, he said, but the fifty thousand-man increase over the regular size of the army. Also, thirty thousand of these were Indians, who would operate on one tenth the cost. Which left twenty thousand men to be accounted for, and if that figure was too high, then the army would reluctantly send those two thousand or so who exceeded the announced cost home. At this, a senator from Missouri said the hearing should keep in mind that the cost of two thousand men was insignificant when compared to the wealth the prairies would bring to the entire nation. In the end, it was determined to recall one thousand men.

Then, like the riots running away from the control of the labor leaders, the hearing ran away from the senators. The final witness was Carl Schurz, the famous German immigrant and founder of the Liberal Republican Party. Because of his reputation as the nation's conscience, he would give the hearing the stamp of truth; and because he was now from Missouri, close to the action, he could be relied on to be friendly.

"From sources in the army," Schurz said, "I have learned that the cost of operating a regiment not 'actively' but in action would be, including horses, pay, and weaponry, four times the amount disclosed by the Department of War. My experience as an officer in a number of armies including your own agrees with this second estimate, which means the cost of this seventy-five thousand–man army would be one billion six hundred seventy-two thousand dollars." He went on with Teutonic thoroughness detailing the expenses as the witnesses from the War Department exchanged despairing looks with the committee chairman. When the people read the headlines the next day it wasn't about the play act for one thousand soldiers but of the incredible sum an impoverished nation was being asked to pay out for the Railroad War.

The protest to the "price of a train ticket," as *Harper's Weekly* put it, gathered strength like an avalanche, especially when the Democrats jumped on the issue with both feet. Out of nowhere they had an issue to club Hayes with and they meant to use it. New Senate hearings were scheduled with a vehemence. Officers were summoned to testify on the expense of putting down previous Indian uprisings. The first witness divulged that the fifty Modoc who rebelled a few years earlier had cost the United States Army forty dead, ninety wounded, and one million dollars. The committee dragged out of oblivion a Senate report made only two years earlier on the Apache Extermination Policy, which said:

". . . the Americans adopted the Mexican theory of extermination and by acts of inhuman treachery and cruelty make them implacable foes. . . . This policy has resulted in a war which in the last ten years has cost us a thousand lives and forty million dollars, and the country is no quieter nor the Indians any nearer extermination."

On the subject of any wealth the Great Plains might mean to the nation, the hearing reminded newspaper readers that until a short time ago the Plains were called the Great American Desert and that it had been termed unfit for habitation by any other than Indians. Homesteading began in earnest after the war and already in '73 the first great drought had hit the area. It was unfit for agriculture, testified John Wesley Powell, and he added that "stock grazing is causing even more injury to the grasslands than the farmer."

Pursuing the theme of economy, they revived a '65 congressional report that said:

". . . the blunders and want of discretion of inexperienced officers in command have brought on long and expensive wars. . . . Since we acquired New Mexico, the military expenditures have probably exceeded four million dollars annually in that region alone. When General Sumner was in command of that department he recommended the purchase of all the private property of citizens and the surrender of that whole territory to the Indians, and upon the score of economy it would doubtless have been a great saving to the government."

The implication was that it was perhaps not so terrible that the Indians seize the territory without having the government responsible for reimbursement. It was not lost on the public.

The White House counterattacked. Stories of atrocities increased despite the questions by senators as to what whites were left in the Indian territory to outrage. Honor was at stake. Borders were no longer secure; the Mexicans or Canadians might step in any time and take over. It would be protecting the Indians themselves to attack before somebody else did.

The Quakers entered the fray, ridiculing the government's logic and affronting Hayes by establishing an Indian Rights Association in Philadelphia. They argued for a new general treaty with the Indians that would be incorporated into the Constitution. The Society of Friends didn't really believe that the Indians would be able to succeed in setting up a separate government.

A Century of Dishonor became a best seller. Its author was Helen Hunt Jackson, an avid Indian sympathizer. She listed the long line of discarded treaties.

People around the world were thrilled by the romantic notion of Rousseau's warriors taking on modern society. Darwin and Huxley, who together berated the British government for its severity in putting down the Jamaica slave revolt, sent a letter to the White House appealing for mercy for the Indian. The letter was signed by over seven thousand British subjects from all walks of life. Prime Minister Disraeli offered his services as mediator between the United States and the Indians. Hayes reminded Disraeli that the Monroe Doctrine excluded European nations from meddling in the New World. Disraeli replied that it was Monroe who said that between the Mississippi and California "there is a vast territory to which the Indians might be invited with inducements that might be successful."

The fact that Britain, Germany, France, Belgium, and Russia all took the same general tone to the war did not strike the United States government as odd. The Czar, for example, cited his country's role in settling America as reason for his concern for the Indians. At the same time, Alexander was busy crushing the Tower to the People Socialists with torture and murder. It was usual for nations to be more libertarian in foreign affairs than at home.

It was remarkable when Marx and monarchs agreed on something, though. A former correspondent for the *Tribune*, the German expatriate wrote long letters to friends, saying, "I thought the Revolution was going to come from a cannon, not an arrow. I wish Greeley were alive. He would have sent me to the battlefronts in an instant."

While the Wasichu world argued over history, the Indians continued to shape their forces. With the Pacific peoples, the Savane of Oklahoma, those who came by way of Canada, and the ones brought by Sheridan, the population of the Indian Nation was over two hundred thousand with a fighting force half that size. The Mormons added another ten thousand soldiers.

Camps larger than any ever seen before were springing up on the prairies. Cherokee log cabins sat beside Crow tipis bright with colored ribbons and Lakota tipis spangled with scalps. A visitor could within a hundred yards pass by the wood and earth lodges of Hidatsa, the grass lodges of Wichita, and an Omaha camp of snugly bundled planks. Tsitsistas and Iroquois discovered that the other played lacrosse and hundred-player games were organized outside the camp. Every Plains tribe adopted a new-coming nation and was responsible for teaching it customs and sign language.

In an impressive ceremony viewed by thousands, the Pawnee returned to the Tsitsistas the two sacred arrows they had captured forty-six years before. Cherokee and Pawnee spent quieter days walking over the grass, choosing places where corn would grow best. Children of all the nations followed their hero They Fear His Horses until he gave up and played with them as he always did.

Lakota women bustled to the tipi of Laughs A Lot, a young warrior. Inside, his wife Saw Rainbows was giving birth to a squalling red boy. The two godmothers chosen for their good nature took charge. One cut and tied the umbilical cord, then cleaned out the baby's mouth with her finger. The second wiped off the baby's body with the inside bark of a chokecherry that had been soaked and beaten soft. When he was dry, they covered the boy with grease and red paint. Over his bottom was wrapped a diaper of the softest buckskin that contained a powder of dried buffalo chips.

Laughs A Lot was sitting in apparent casual conversation with a pair of friends near the tipi. One of the godmothers opened the flap of the tipi. "You have a boy. He's good and strong. As ugly as you right now but he'll look better tomorrow. Saw Rainbows is fine."

Laughs A Lot tried to think of a retort, but his mind stopped working and he leaned back, laughing with delight.

In another camp far to the west in Idaho, an ancient chief of the avaricious, slave-owning Maklaks shared the wealth he had escaped with among poor Tlingit and Haida. Over the plains, Shawnee and Mohawk rode with Siksika learning how to hunt Issiwun, the buffalo. Warrior societies welcomed the Savane veterans with ceremonies that lasted for weeks.

They would bring back the old ways, they kept saying to each other. But the old ways were dead. They belonged to primitive hunting communities and the Indians, quite suddenly, were no longer that.

Two weeks had passed with five meetings between Holds Eagles and the president and his staff. After each one, the White House sent a message to Camp of the Nations asking whether Holds Eagles's bewildering array of half-offers was authorized by the Council of Chiefs, and each time the Council replied that they were.

"I have to admit, you're keeping them off balance," Liz said.

It was evening and they were walking through the security gate of an apartment house from the parking lot. Television cameras followed them through the lobby and another picked them up in the elevator.

"Merely exploring all possible avenues of peaceful coexistence," Holds Eagles said.

The hostess was waiting for them at the door. Her eyes were

gleaming as brightly as the stones around her neck. Inside, the capital's elite were waiting with poorly concealed eagerness for the catch of the social season.

Marsha Manne kissed Liz and laid a hand gently on Holds Eagles's arm. "You're even younger than you look on television. Everyone is waiting to meet you."

"They look like they're wetting their pants, from the chief justice on down," Liz whispered. "You're being seen, all right."

Holds Eagles mingled with the partygoers right away. He knew that they were here on the sly and that they couldn't resist the opportunity. It reminded him of that line from Shakespeare, "They will not give a doit to relieve a poor beggar, but they will lay out ten to see a dead Indian."

"I don't mind admitting that there's supposed to be some Cherokee in my family way back," the chief justice said. "So maybe I have more than a little sympathy."

Holds Eagles asked how the justice saw the legality of the border problem.

"The hitch is, for you, that there is no title to the land. If it were private property, that would be different."

"You're stalling," a columnist said. "Something's happening, something your scientists are working up. Bacteria. Must be something like that when you talk about 'terrible costs.' All the luck in the world to you," he said as he reached for another drink.

"How did you get such a fascinating name? Did your family call you that?" the daughter of a senator asked.

"You could say that I dreamed it up myself."

"I hope I never meet you in a poker game," an admiral said. "I've seen sweet bluffs in my time but nothing like the one you're pulling. That's the Indian straight face for you."

"We're having a sort of kaffeeklatsch on Friday," an artist's wife said, "and we were wondering whether you could take an hour off and explain the Indian situation to us. In depth, I mean. The girls have some influence."

"My children are very excited about this prospect of war with the Indians," a mother said. "I think they're even more excited than they were about Vietnam."

"She's right," the father said. "God, they dress like Indians, live like Indians. Their friends are the same way. Do your kids dress like us?"

"I suppose this violence thing is getting to you," a sociologist said. "But we're a violent society, perhaps the most violent that ever existed."

"The things they used to say at school about Indian men," an unhappy wife sighed wisely. "The myths you hear as a girl. I couldn't help but wonder if you used to hear the same things about white women."

"How did you get your name? I forgot to ask you that," Liz said as they drove to Georgetown in the early morning breeze. A justice car followed a block behind.

"Same as anyone else. I had a vision. I was particularly eager to have mine because as a kid I was called Running Nose. Seriously, I had an allergy problem and a sarcastic father."

"So you had a vision." She let her head fall back on the seat and watched tree branches whip overhead.

"Long story."

"I've never heard how someone gets their name through a vision before."

"Okay. My family was Choctaw but it had been adopted some time ago by the Tsitsistas, Cheyenne to you. We did things their way. Which meant when I was thirteen and complaining about my name, I was taken by my grandfather to see a wicha-sha, a priest, a nice old man who asked me some questions and said I was ready for a vision. The very next day he came by our tipi—aluminum and ash, two stories, I should add—and said a place was ready for me on the high buttes. I picked out my best pony and rode out with just a parfleche of jerky and made myself a little camp there the first night.

"I dreamed a lot but I didn't have any visions. It would have been odd if I had. You have to fast at least two days before you're in the right state. So I did. No food, water just three times a day."

"Are we talking about visions or hallucinations?" Liz asked.

Holds Eagles laughed. "It depends whether you're Indian or Wasichu. Anyway, I must have been particularly unimaginative, because after four days I still hadn't seen a damn thing besides some ants. My father was about to say the hell with it and pick me up, but on the fifth night I got what I came for.

"I thought I was still awake. As a matter of fact, everything was as clear or clearer than what you'd call reality. There was a buzzard overhead, high up in the dark, but for some reason I could see it and I knew that it could see me. In the state I was in, lying on that rock, I must have seemed like a steak dinner to it, and I started cursing the whole stupid idea of the vision. I threw a rock up at it, as if I could throw a rock a mile, which I couldn't.

"It disappeared. I was scared sick because I felt better when I could see it. Then there was a blast of wind and a sort of muffled clatter of wings. There was a sickening odor, too, I remember that. I managed to turn over and there he was, the biggest, vilest buzzard you'd ever lay eyes on, a foot away! I tried dragging myself away on my back but he took one hop and landed on my chest with the weight of a horse, sticking his beak and eyes down into my face. Do you want me to go on?"

"I certainly don't want to leave you in that predicament," Liz said.

"It gets worse. He was too heavy. He just sat there leering at me while I screamed for my father to come and shoot the bird. Dad was nowhere around. So the buzzard started going to work. First, he plucked my eyes out, one by one as if they were grapes. Then he ripped my chest open and ate my heart, and then he lowered his aim and ate my testicles. I was not aware of a great deal of pain but I was terrified and humiliated. Even if I couldn't see, I somehow knew that he was looking me over, seeing if there was anything else worth gobbling up. Apparently there wasn't because he started to take off.

"That was when I grabbed him. One thing a buzzard doesn't do well is take off, very clumsy at that. It was outraged that a dead boy should hold it down and it pecked away at me, just about leaving a skeleton, while it flapped away trying to get some altitude. I still hung on out of pure spite and the buzzard finally broke its wing on the rock. That was it. A buzzard with a broken wing is a dead bird. It sat down beside me, much quieter, and said, okay, I'd won, and that he would trade me the broken wing for my eyes."

Liz's head shot off the seat. "He spoke to you?"

"That's what I said. It was a wing for the eyes. I said no, and he thought about it and came back with another offer, the wing for my heart. No. At last he offered the wing for my testicles. No, again. I'm not going to bore you with the haggling that went on all night but we went through all the combinations of eyes and heart for the wing. The bird was very put out that I dared to bargain about these points, but at sunrise he gave in. My eyes, heart, and testicles, good as new, plus whatever flesh I had lost, in exchange for the broken wing. I agreed. So when my father came by an hour later, the buzzard was gone and I was the same as I started, except for losing ten pounds of baby fat."

"Hold it. You're called Holds Eagles, not Holds Buzzards. Where did the switch come in?"

He glanced in the rear-view mirror just to check if the car was still trailing them and went on.

"After I got home. I told my family and the wichasha what happened on the rock four or five times so that I wouldn't leave anything out. The priest was very mystified. It turned out that the bird I always described was an eagle, although I thought of him as a buzzard. This is important because the eagle is very sacred to all the tribes of the Plains. You don't just go around calling him a buzzard. A bunch of the wichasha got together and decided that either I was lying, insulting the medicine of the eagle—a bad boy's trick—or I was telling the truth as I saw it. The only way I could prove it was by catching an eagle."

"How do you go about that?"

"Wait and learn. It's quite simple but not the sort of thing a boy does. It's for an older man. Usually. Anyway, my father and grandfather stuck by me and the three of us drove out in our panel truck to a place where eagles were numerous. We waited until there were none in the sky and then, as quickly as we could, we dug a pit big enough for me to sit. When it was done, we put a false roof of long grass over it and drove miles away to dump the dirt. Eagles are very sharp-eyed and suspicious creatures.

"I stayed up all night singing eagle songs with my father's help, ending up with a sweat bath and a coating of eagle-grease paint. Then we drove back to the pit so I could get in it before dawn when the eagles would be flying. My father fastened the bait into the grass and left.

"There's only one way you are allowed to kill an eagle, strangling it with a noose so that as few of his feathers as possible are broken. My father was an expert and he taught me as much as he could, but I don't think I did anything in that pit for hours but look up through my peephole and cry. You see, an adult eagle has a wingspread of seven feet, a beak like an axe, and talons.

It was very unlikely that I would even be able to pull one down into the pit with me once I grabbed hold of his leg. I was looking forward to a long life being known as One Hand. I was thinking about that prospect when the pit went dark and I heard the eagle tearing at the bait.

"It was dusk when my father and grandfather showed up with the wichasha, and I'm sure they all expected to collect what was left of me. The place was a mess. The eagle had ripped me right out of that carefully prepared pit and about five feet into the air. When we crashed he whacked me in the skull with his beak so that bits of scalp were thrown all over the ground. Then we dragged each other all over the neighborhood, the eagle generally on top while I lost the noose half a dozen times. Luckily, he got carried away with his work on my stomach and I slapped the noose on. It was not a neat job, but it did the trick. A least, my father had no complaints. And that's how I got my name."

They pulled up in front of her house, a shuttered colonial townhouse like every other one on the tree-lined street. Their shadow parked at the corner.

"Long story, I warned you," Holds Eagles said.

"It explains a lot," she said. "Like why I saw you get a dozen sexual propositions back at the party. How would you respond to one more?"

Chapter Five

I will go to the Indian Territory!

—Rutherford Hayes

Hayes followed Sheridan's plan. Leading a new army by himself was the only way the Republican Party would keep the White House, his supporters told him. The congressional elections for the year promised to be a disaster anyway.

The fact that Sheridan had been held in inactivity during the winter of '77-'78 seemed to be an opportunity. Mustering another thirty thousand men to replace the missing Indians, Hayes set off after fame and the Indian in the long tradition of Washington, Jackson, Harrison, even Lincoln. The world was galvanized at the sight of the president astride a black charger reviewing his army on the Kansas fields. Nobody could deny that he had been a game, if uninspired, general in the Civil War.

Logistical encampments followed the army like footprints as it moved through Colorado in the second week of May. The staff considered it a good sign that no Indians had been sighted and that telegraphic communications to the encampments and the East were unimpaired. To the host of reporters, it meant drawing lots for time on the wires. Hayes received news of the GAR rallies that were being held for him in every city in the North.

On May 20 a long message came over the wire. At first only the decoder was listening. In minutes, the room was crowded. It was from Sitting Bull, sending from someplace behind them. He offered Hayes terms of unconditional surrender. To reporters he offered the chance to ride with the Indian forces. All they had to do was ride out of camp in any direction, he said, and they would be welcomed. For the first time, an eerie sensation pervaded the expedition. Hayes put out orders against it but a few of the more adventurous correspondents sneaked out of camp that evening.

It was thanks to them that the world first learned of what took place on May 30, on the buttes of Mchweaming, called Wyoming. There was no ambush, no sneak attack by the Indians. They were there watching as Hayes and his cavalry point rode up the Yellow Buttes.

"Lord God, well here they are," General de Trobriand, second-in-command, said.

Hayes was looking through his field glasses. He had never seen so many Indians in his life, and he suspected that nobody else had, either.

"Who are they?" he asked his scout.

The scout spun slowly in his saddle as he looked through the glasses. "Who aren't they. Blackfoot, Crow, Arapahoe, many Sioux, many Cheyenne. I see a hell of a lot in white dress, maybe the civilized tribes, Chippewa, Osage, more. Many more. I can't see them all."

"They're in military formation," de Trobriand said. "All cavalry."

"I see cannons," the scout said. "Did you tell them where we were going to be?"

"They're usually cavalry from what I hear," Hayes said. "How many would you guess?"

"Thirty thousand, forty," de Trobriand said. "Just waiting for us to do something."

Hayes slapped his bugler on the arm.

They Fear His Horses looked down at the officers riding back to their troops. He had no war bonnet on, only a spotted eagle feather hanging down between the braids of his hair. When he saw the army troops move forward, he dismounted and scooped some dirt off the ground. He smudged some of it first on the pony's head between the ears and then on the flanks. Spilling dirt into his other hand as if it were a magic dust to be measured out, he walked to the front of the horse and threw some in back and in front, making sure some landed on the pony's head. Finally, he rubbed the rest of the earth off the pony and onto his face. He never wore face paint into battle.

"All you brave warriors who have to move their bowels from fear better do it now," he said as he started riding up and down the lines. His society of last born, the Ho-ksi-ha-ka-ta, insulted him in return when they saw him coming, asking if he was leaving already.

Sitting Bull and the wichasha of other nations stood on a butte covered with red dust. The Tsitsistas and Pawnee priests pointed their sacred arrows at the Wasichu soldiers scurrying about into a defensive position below. A pointed buffalo skull peered with them. When the magic was done, the mile-long lines whooped in a noise that made the chaplains giving absolution below look up.

The warrior societies began their war songs; Kit Fox, Crooked Lances, Crazy Dogs, Red Shields, Chief Soldiers, Horn, Buffalo

Bull, Dog Soldiers of many nations, and a hundred other societies behind so that the air was full of men's voices, even of the Cherokee, singing "Onward Christian Soldiers."

"This is your day," Wovoka told John Setter on the hill. The Paiute prophet had traded in his overalls for the white buckskin leggings of the Siksika.

"You know something, you're right," Setter said as he left the hill of priests for the line of Ho-ksi-ha-ka-ta. "I wouldn't miss this for the world."

Dirt and grass exploded in front of the lines from army cannon. Dog Soldiers patrolled the ranks keeping discipline. The Wasichu's formation was a square within a box with three sides. One side was made up of Savane with Stand Watie in command, the other side made of Tsitsistas, Siksika, and other plains nations under Two Moons, and the bottom was solid Lakota led by They Fear His Horses.

At his signal, the Cherokee howitzer batteries opened fire with explosive shells. In their secure defensive position, outnumbering their enemy three to one, Hayes and his officers wondered if the Indians would have the nerve to attack, when the center of their square began erupting in fountains of dirt, wagons, and horses. De Trobriand was the first to realize what was happening.

"The field is mined, booby trapped," he said. "It's a Prussian trick."

Incoming shells added to the confusion as Hayes desperately tried to get his army moving again. Stand Watie raised his arm and the Savane line moved forward. The soldiers' Springfields gave them superior range, but on the rolling buttes they never had the Indians in range long enough before the line of cavalry burst on top of them with their Winchester repeaters.

Hayes bravely led a counterattack himself with the Sixth

Cavalry as the Savane veered away. As the soldiers came near, a regiment of Lenape and Potawatomi stopped in their tracks and formed a square of four levels, lying down, kneeling, standing, and mounted, the way these two nations had been fighting as mercenaries for years. The soldiers found themselves riding in a circle around the square as the Savane guns volleyed in order without a stop, rank by rank. Indians would have slid on the other side or under their ponies, but the soldiers couldn't. They fell like insects, until Hayes ordered a retreat.

Two Moons's ten thousand raced past the square after the Wasichu's left flank. The Potawatomi were busily dipping bullets in Wasichu blood. A company of Crow with cedar bows fired grenades into the fleeing soldiers whenever officers tried to make them halt. By now They Fear His Horses and the Lakota had joined the chase, riding over three regiments of the Fourth Cavalry, unloading the magazines of their rifles amid the yells of "Hokahey" and the favorite war cry of the Dog Soldiers, "It's a great day for dying!"

The army was too large to stampede as easily as that, however. De Trobriand had Gatlings set on wagons and cut down a charge by the Kit Foxes. Major James was making sense out of the infantry, getting them comfortable on their stomachs. Colonel Arnold reformed the Fourth and Fifth Cavalry under fire and led them in a charge with one purpose: to kill They Fear His Horses.

On the Hill of Women, they almost did it. They Fear His Horses was wandering around the butte looking for a pony to take the place of the one just shot from under him. Arnold and a hundred men of the Fifth raced up toward the chief. On top of the hill were the five sacred homosexuals, the Contraries, of the Tsitsistas. The Contrary is, by nature, a suicidal warrior, extremely courageous and hard to kill, allowed to carry a magic lance he may not use for fighting. A Contrary who does so must die in the combat, so the Contraries knew what they were doing when they rode down to meet Arnold's hundred.

At first the soldiers didn't know what to make of the five braves so eager to clash with them. Then the Contraries were among the soldiers, slashing out with the lances as their ponies rode down the larger army horses. They didn't have to aim a gun and there was no lack of targets, so the Contraries simply waded through the horse soldiers without a thought to the hideous wounds they were receiving. When their lances broke, they seized rifles from soldiers, and when the rifles were empty they used them as clubs. By the time the last of them was killed, more than thirty saddles of the Fifth were empty and They Fear His Horses was mounted, leading an enraged thousand Lakota in a charge that swept through James's defenses to the Gatlings, which they captured and turned on the soldiers. De Trobriand was captured along with a number of other staff officers. At this point, Hayes had suffered fewer than two thousand casualties and the Indians about three hundred-fifty, leaving him with the enormous numerical advantage he started with. It was hard to believe that the battle was lost, but it was.

The army was on the run, reeling from the steady cavalry charges of the enemy, demoralized and without its best commander. Hayes was unable to make sense of the Indian force of pure horsemen. When he tried to bring his infantry into play, the Cherokee batteries zeroed in on them and were driving wagons with Gatlings over the soldiers who tried to stand and fight. President Hayes decided to retreat as orderly as possible to the first high ground.

It was the first of many retreats in a drama that the American public lived through with its leader. The Indians made sure of that. Controlling the telegraph, they let the correspondents send a full description of each day's action. It usually consisted of a surrender plea by Sitting Bull refused by Hayes, some ambushed sorties by the latter's cavalry, and a night of shelling for the US camp. Hayes managed to lose about five hundred men a day in dubious attempts to break out of the Indian ring. Sitting Bull told the correspondents that he wished Congress would call the president back so that no more men on either side would be mourned by their families. He reminded them that all the action had been in Indian territory, that he only wanted to defend his own land and not invade the United States. He treated his prisoners of war well and let them send greetings to their mothers.

"Who are you?" the *New York World* asked John Setter.

"My name is Where The Sun Goes," Setter said.

"You seem to be a chief with some, uh, heap big power around here. Could you tell us what you expect the white soldiers to do?"

"We expect President Hayes to make a desperate dash to Kansas."

"Oh."

Hayes made his doomed dash. To begin with, an Indian pony could beat any army horse over a short distance. Over a long distance, the pony subsisted happily on grass while the army horse needed grain. Most important, the Indians traveled with huge herds of horses so that they could constantly relay the ones they were riding. The US Cavalry rode on one mount the whole time. After two days the Indians had cut off five thousand stragglers at will and the army was staggering.

On June 12 two more bits of news from the Indians staggered the United States. Sheridan's expedition of five thousand in New Mexico had ended in the desert, almost completely wiped out by the ten thousand Apache, Kiowa, Comanche, Pima, and Yuma lead by He Who Yawns, Victorio, and Black Horse. In the end, the soldiers had been reduced to cutting their wrists for something to drink, not the first time this horror had happened to men serving in the dunes against Goy-ya-thle.

From Nevada came the news of the San Francisco Volunteers, a seven thousand–man militia raised by Denis Kearney, the Teamster leader who fought the immigration of Chinese. Kearney and thirty-five hundred were dead, whipped by the Paiute, Ute, Shoshone, and Nauvoo Legion.

The following day the council of chiefs made their "Appeal to the American People." They said that the army under President Hayes was gallant but that it was defeated, that further fighting could only end in a massacre of the troops that the Indians wanted no part of. In the interest of humanity, they pleaded with the American people to ask President Hayes to let his soldiers lay down their arms and return home safely. President Hayes, they added, would be escorted home with all the honors due a chief of state.

In Washington, the Democrats pushed for a congressional ultimatum to Hayes that he negotiate. The Republican majority stopped the bill, but the majority of the people had made up their minds. Hayes had stolen the White House, shot down citizens in almost every major city, and now he was taking the United States to its worst military defeat over a land nobody wanted. When the War Department and the army said that the middle of the continent could never be given up for reasons of security, people said to each other that with the sort of generals the army had, the only secure border was someplace in the middle of Asia.

"With the moral commitment, the spirit, and the leadership of the War Between the States, we could have romped over the presumptuous braves in a month," Grant said. "This fight is not over because America will not betray her citizens on the edge of the frontier, the very edge of civilization," read a document distributed by representatives of the western states. "Christian civilization is at stake," Archbishop McCloskey and the Knights of the White Camellia said on the same day.

Three weeks after he had first met the Indians on the Yellow Buttes, President Hayes rode out of his camp to meet his enemy under a flag of truce. A tipi midway between the forces was set up. Accompanying Hayes were two major generals and a secretary. Representing the Indians were Sitting Bull, Stand Watie, Where The Sun Goes, and a Shawnee school teacher to take notes.

"It is over," a rider screamed as he jumped his horse over a cannon, spreading the good news.

The long line of Wasichu were marching down from the butte to the east, leaving the hill covered with their rifles, cartridge crates, and howitzers. The rider went on from Cherokee to Iroquois with the good news, and when all the warriors of the nations were cheering, he switched ponies to ride to the great home camp so that wives and mothers and children could prepare for the celebrations.

The warriors prepared by stopping a mile from the camp of their families. If none had been killed, the Lakota would have led the way with ash-darkened faces, but a thousand men had died in the war and that special rejoicing was denied. Dog Soldiers instructed jubilant Savane in the proper conduct of victory so that all was done well. Instead of human scalps, since Wovoka and They Fear His Horses had decreed that this had not been a fight for sport, they wore streamers made of horsehair. Tsitsistas dried deer hide drums in the sun while Seneca added the snapping turtle rattles they had brought across Canada and Pawnee made bullroarers. All the young men cut their best-looking ponies from the enormous milling herds.

All the people in the polyglot metropolis of tipis, lodges, and cabins gathered at its eastern end, gazing at a hill. A regiment of Lakota seemed to spring from it, their ceremonial lance ribbons fluttering in the air as they charged down at the camp. A regiment of Pawnee came next, then Cherokee in bright red shirts, more Lakota, Tsitsistas, Siksika, more regiments, an unending stream of them on waves of dust, all calling in unison, "Hown, hown!" The rolling, color-brilliant charge broke to the left of the spectators who cried in reply, "Hi-yay, hi-yay!" The warriors took their hands from the reins and guided their ponies with their knees so that they could raise their rifles high above their heads and shoot off a string of shells, enough to shoot out the stars. The stream rose off the hill, still spewing more Lakota and Chippewa; Crow wearing crowns of feathers; Mohawk in black suits, Inuna-Ina wearing blouses of scalps, Assiniboin societies with faces quartered into red, blue, yellow, and green; Lenape in leather jackets, Choctaw in corduroy leggings belted in Pueblo silver; naked Arikara, Wazhazhe, Ponca, Muskogee, as if they were being born anew.

>><<

"I always thought of Indians as musclebound. You're not that way. Smooth and cool like copper."

She traced his back with her finger as he bent over the Sunday papers. He finished with the *Star* and began on the *Times*. Liz looked over his shoulder at a picture of the two of them captioned "Constant Companions."

"Does it say that you won me with your stories?" she asked.

"Is that how you think of us, as Othello and Desdemona?" he said, breaking his concentration.

"You know the story?"

"Must you speak of one that loved not wisely but too well? Of one whose hand, like the base Indian, threw a pearl away richer than all his tribe?"

"I see you do." She lit a cigarette nervously. "Then think of me as an over-age beauty."

"Or a land of milk and honey, as any good Mormon would say." He took the cigarette from her mouth.

In another part of town, President Nielson stepped out of a shower and dried himself furiously with a terrycloth towel. Ginny Nielson watched her husband with concern.

"Don, you took a shower before church. Why are you taking another one?"

"It's that damn Indian. They have such a keen sense of smell. I keep having the feeling that he can smell me whenever we talk."

"Nonsense; no one can smell you. If I can't smell you how could anyone else?"

Nielson shook his head in disgust and sprayed his underarms. "I can't impress someone if they can smell me, can I?" he said and squeezed a double wad of toothpaste onto his electric toothbrush.

"That man's upsetting you. I don't like it," Mrs. Nielson said. "It's been almost a month now and he's still got you going around the mulberry bush. Can't you just call the whole thing off?" She walked into the bathroom brushing steam from her face and sat on the toilet. "I'm just amazed that you and Harry can't take care of one Indian."

He spit a mouthful of suds into the sink. "He keeps coming up with things, hints that we might do one thing one day and another thing the next. The press eats it up and then he goes and talks at the UN. A lot is at stake; we can't take any chances. How are underdeveloped countries going to develop if they start listening to the Indians?" He poured a dose of mouthwash down his throat.

"Well?"

A stream of mouthwash splashed into the sink. "Well, if we just throw him in jail that's not going to impress them, either."

"And what about students? I can't turn on the news without hearing about some new riot of theirs. Hasn't Harry got any ideas?"

"He's working on something." The president plucked a hair from his nostril.

Ginny Nielson exhaled dramatically. "I wish you spent as much time getting ready for me as you do for this savage."

"Don't start up on that, Ginny, please," the president said. He unreeled a foot of dental floss and smiled broadly into the mirror.

Chapter Six

Our manifest destiny is to overspread the oceans
allotted by Providence for the free development of
our yearly multiplying millions.

—*US Magazine* and *Democratic Review*

I circle around,
I circle around,
The boundaries of the earth,
The boundaries of the earth,
Wearing the long wing feathers as I fly,
Wearing the long wing feathers as I fly!

—Inuna-Ina

Where does a tidal wave turn to a wave and then merely
a ripple and then die away?" the American historian
Commager has asked. "If the United States had not
lost the inner continent to the Indian Nation, what would the
effect have been on American history?

"Obviously, our energies would have been consumed in taming a new frontier, work that would have lasted perhaps a hundred years.

"The very change of a map means so much. It was not only that we did away with the Indian names for towns and states and lakes, renaming Chicago and calling it Sheridan or making Nebraska Lincoln. Our vision of the world would have been different, inner rather than outer directed. Different leaders might have inspired us to different goals. Presuming that history is not the fixed course most people take it for, would we have had the same roll call of presidents?

"Would Teddy Roosevelt have been able to win the White House on the strength of a few futile raids on the Indians with his Roughriders? Or Admiral Dewey with the naval battle that made the Philippines and Cuba members of the Union?

"If the Battle of Hastings was the greatest turning point in English history, surely the same must be said for the Battle of Yellow Buttes in our own."

The turning point was not accepted with grace by the United States for a long time. No treaty was signed until the Agreement of Sacramento at the end of World War I, which institutionalized the boundaries agreed to by Hayes before his battered army was allowed to wander home. In it, the United States acknowledged that the Indians had voluntarily returned control of Nevada and Oklahoma. The Western United States thus consisted of Nevada, California, Oregon, and Washington. The western border of the Eastern United States was Texas, Oklahoma, Kansas, Nebraska, a corner of Iowa, and Minnesota. When demands for reparations were made by the US, the Indians countered with reparation demands of their own, triple that of the US. The matter was dropped.

To Americans, the new nation in their midst was a paradox.

It was now regarded as inevitable that the tribes would unite, and that as a united force they would be unbeatable. Government studies proved this at great length, comparing the cumbersome machine of a US regiment with its slow infantry, its wagons of pork, salt meat, flour, peas, sugar, coffee, vinegar, soap, and tallow, to the free-moving Indians content with parched corn and jerked beef. Drafting procedures were contrasted to the religious fervor and combative upbringing of Indian volunteers. Indian ponies were incomparably suited for plains fighting, and the plains made up a terrain perfect for a purely cavalry army.

At the same time, no Americans were yet convinced that the Indians would be able to govern themselves. Daily reports said that anarchy and starvation were sweeping the nations, that Sitting Bull and the Sioux controlled other Indians through intimidation, that a man called Where the Sun Goes was actually white and was operating for any number of foreign powers.

Gradually, though, the United States turned its mind and its face in other directions.

And, in 1880, as a last attempt to win the respect of the voters, Hayes and the Republicans suddenly ratified the treaty on the grounds that a foreign power was about to purchase the Bay of Samaná. As Admiral MacMahon said, "This step into the oceans means nothing without a navy to make use of it. Without a great navy, the United States must reconcile itself to always being a second-rate power." The great navy followed as the nation expanded outwards into the seas behind a line of energetic admirals. The Panama Canal was built for necessary communications with the western half of the Union, forestalling concern that it would secede. Spain was pushed from Cuba and the Philippines, and annexation procedures rushed through an active Congress. Hawaii, Alaska, and Puerto Rico were next so that by the start of WWI, the United States could look out on

Atlantic and Pacific empires guarded by an active sea force as large as Great Britain's.

In the meantime, America's hopes that the Indian Nation would fall apart in dissension were almost coming true. With the war over, the instinct of the nations was to return to their old lands and the enjoyment of their old ways. They didn't know that those old ways were dead. The most that they would agree to, particularly the Inde under He Who Yawns, was the contribution of regiments from each tribe to a common border patrol. Setter had more success with the Siksika, the Savane, and other tribes who were new to the area claimed by the Indian Nation. They were much more willing to adapt to the demands of the country that had adopted them. Telegraph networks, schools, and a census were conducted largely by the Savane. Setter bided time for the older chiefs to pass on so that the reorganization of the nation could start.

Time didn't wait. General Philippe Regis Denis de Kereden de Trobriand, the former prisoner of war, was the new representative of the European consortium. They had equipped the Indian army and now they wanted the return on their investment, meaning the control of all mineral, fur, and timber rights, along with management and development of steamship and railroad lines. De Trobriand, son of a baron, lawyer, famous in his home France for "Quatre Ans de Campagnes a l'Armee du Potomac," was hired to make the most of the situation. When he found Sitting Bull under Setter's influence, he turned to dividing the nations against themselves.

The Inde Rebellion began in 1880. De Trobriand had paid He Who Yawns's Chiricahua to open a railroad line to Mexico. Setter led an army of Savane to New Mexico and spoke to Victorio. The old Mimbreno chief agreed that action was necessary but he refused to lead his men against his longtime companion.

The Rebellion ended in '81 on a canyon slope much like the one Setter and He Who Yawns had first met on years before. A mountain stream gushed through the rocks to go underground a thousand feet below. He Who Yawns was lying in the shade of a boulder with his life seeping from a grenade wound in his chest.

"It's nice, you know, here," he said to Setter, who ripped a shirt to bandage him. "It's the way I wanted to go. Don't argue with me, don't tell me that I was doing wrong. I should have gone along, I knew. But we won, you said we won, and when we came back here to our home to be Inde, all of a sudden you wanted us to start acting like them, the whites. We just wanted to be left alone. That's why we fought to begin with. Then you wanted our men to go north, west, away from home. That wasn't the old way, that's not what we fought for. The whites always wanted to send us here and there to fight; that's what we didn't like. Then we win and we find out that win or lose it's all the same. You will have to forgive us if we were confused. We thought we were fighting for something else. Well, I'm dying here and that's not so bad. If I lived, I'd have to live your way and, frankly, I think it smells. I die this way, the old way, and I'm happy. Did I fight well?"

"You always fight well," Setter said.

"Good. Well, if you'll forgive me, I'll try to forgive you," Goy-ya-thle said, and then he was dead, just a bow-legged, wiry man with gray hair who was called "the worst Indian who ever lived." Setter dressed the small figure in a jacket patterned with bright beads as the four winds to hide the shattered chest. On his head he put a cap with pronged antelope horns to carry the spirit on a run to the spirit world.

De Trobriand next tried the Mormons. On the west flank of the country, wondering when they would be asked to take charge of the whole country, President Taylor's Latter-Day Saints were becoming uneasy. The Sons of Laman were showing little zeal in sharing control of the land. De Trobriand's offer to help restore the Empire of Deseret as it should be was very appealing.

"There are some definite attractions to the Mormon Church," Setter said. He was in Taylor's office. With him were Wovoka and a platoon of Dog Soldiers. With Taylor was the head of the Sons of Dan and a brace of his men. In back was the same large map, except that the large irregular block in the center was painted green and retitled Deseret.

"For instance," Setter went on, "the rebirth of all Latter-Day Saints as opposed to Gentiles. I know you wouldn't have any dealings with Gentiles," he said and paused. "Also, I think the inclusion of the rest of the country of the Sons of Laman is very important. Full participation in religious activities is necessary, I agree."

"Actually," Taylor said, "the Sons of Laman have not yet been cleansed by Mormon. They can't become priests, even should they participate fully. It would take a Revelation for them to be purged officially."

"Who would have that Revelation?"

"God would speak to me."

"Ah," Setter said. He walked around the center of the room as if he were thinking something out. "How long would it take you to receive that Revelation?"

"That's up to God," Taylor said with dignity.

"It seems to me that the Revelation is a little overdue. Here we are, Sons of Laman and Sons of Nephi victorious in our own land just as Moroni said. What more do you want?"

"It's not up to me."

"Up to God, fine. Because we know He will send you that Revelation today. This afternoon. Because if He doesn't, we're burning your City of Zion to the ground. There are forty thousand warriors entering town right now. Take your time."

Taylor dispatched the Danite to see if there was any truth to Setter's statement. From the look on the policeman's face when he came back, the answer was yes. Music was heard through the window and the president dashed to it to see a thick column of Indians armed with rifles marching behind a brass band of Cherokee. A banner held up behind them said "Sons of Laman Day of Conversion." People on the streets were surprised but applauded.

"They'll camp in front of the Tabernacle," Setter said. "Something else. God will very likely tell you that Wovoka, having proved his merit as a prophet, is to be raised to leadership in the Church equal to you. I think that's only right."

"Anything else?" Taylor asked with as much sarcasm as a plain man could muster.

"Yes. I know that you think that Wovoka and I are opportunists, dictating to you behind a gun. Which is true, I assure you. But Wovoka is not an opportunist. He is a prophet and all he has said has come to be. Now I am an opportunist, but it's obvious even to me that the great opportunity here is yours. God has made you triumphant with your brothers, the Indians. Yet you go off making deals like some petty merchant, ignoring what God has given you. The very fact that we have won is a Revelation, and for you to say no leads us to believe that you refuse to listen to God. Mormon has brought us here together today. You can deny his voice and cause the destruction of His city and His disciples or you can listen to him to cause rejoicing throughout Heaven at our great reunion."

"What was that last part all about?" Agate, one of the Dog Soldiers, asked as the Indians went out to wait for Taylor's answer in the corridor. There was no other way for Taylor to leave his office. The Danites were locked in another room so that the president could be alone.

"The last part is known as letting a man think that he wanted all along to do what he wants to do least," Setter said.

"Maybe God really will speak to him," Agate said.

"Exactly."

President Taylor's announcement of March 2, 1881, marked the beginning of Indian Mormonism. It also marked the end of de Trobriand's intrigues in the Indian Nation. The Council of Chiefs told the consortium that they would honor their agreements only if the general were ordered to leave; otherwise, they would kill him.

The consortium, which had operated with such good effect in other parts of the world, was finding that it had little leverage with the Indians. Withholding arms and ammunition was ineffective because the Indians already had a healthy stockpile of delivered and captured weapons. The very first Indian industry was the manufacturing of bullets and shells. It was going on before the Battle of Yellow Buttes. With buffalo being killed only for food and not for furs, the herds were stabilizing. The Cherokee had long been the finest farmers in the country and the Pawnee were expanding their cornfields. Trying to put the squeeze on through hunger wouldn't work, either.

Worst of all, the consortium discovered, simple intimidation, the last resort, was laughed at. They soon found out why. There was no way of threatening the Indian with gunboats with the United States at both seas. When troops were massed along the Canadian border in the summer of '83, Europe found itself facing not only the Indians but an aroused America. Washington didn't like the Indians; technically they were still at war. But the last thing they would put up with was a European power base in trade for an independent Indian country. President Bayard sent a message through the State Department that if the threat to the Indian Nation were carried out, the United States would feel obliged to invade Canada. The Monroe Doctrine was not dead. While the cagey financiers of London and Paris were being outfoxed by the Indians, Americans looked on with wry humor.

"History," as a Wasichu once said, "has a way of repeating itself." To win their revolution, the Americans made a treaty of perpetual friendship with the French against England. Then they broke it after the English were beaten. "We made an agreement with the Europeans to fight the Americans. We will not break our agreement but the Europeans have destroyed our trust so we will give them only things that can help us. The main thing is to keep up their interest so that the Wasichu from Europe and the Wasichu from America will keep their eyes on each other and not on us. It will be greed against greed while we grow strong."

Setter stopped talking so that the chiefs could discuss the idea among themselves. They were seated on fur-covered benches that rose in a ring around him. The wooden, tipi-like structure rose seventy feet in the air with an open center at its peak to admit the sky. It had been built to house the first conference of all the chiefs with wood from every part of the Indian Nation.

"Let me say this," Black Horse said as he stood up. He had changed a lot since the early days of the struggle. The arrogance had changed to quiet confidence; the Sun Dance scars had done that to him. "We understand what you are trying to do for us when you speak to Wasichu. But when you say that we must make some sort of federation of nations like the Wasichu, we wonder. Do we have to be like them so much?"

Setter nodded his head in sympathy and turned to the Seneca. A tall, spectacled man rose.

"The Wasichu copied us," he said in a reedy voice. "The League of the Longhouse was just such a federation. This is very complicated, but I will try to make it simple.

"When the colonies first wanted to unite against their enemies they met in the Convention of Albany, a place in New York. There was much disagreement over which way they should join together. The wisest man there was Franklin and he suggested that they use us, the League, as their model. The colonies were not yet ready to fight, though, and the meeting came to nothing. But a few years later in 1776, they were ready and Franklin again was asked to help make the laws of their federation. Much of what the Wasichu agreed to was only a copy of the League. So you see we would not be copying them, only ourselves."

The Seneca lawyer went on at length about the structure of the League, the peace chiefs and war chiefs, the elections, and the status of women. The audience was impressed. Many points were similar to their own nations', and they exclaimed in delight when this was so. Setter listened and didn't listen. The Seneca suddenly struck him as an Ichabod Crane, not an Indian. And as for himself, he would never be one of them. He might die defending the nation he'd helped create, but his mind would be other places too. In a steamy cassock trudging up the Spanish Steps, making love in a Bolivian cave, of late his mind seemed to demand to travel by itself.

It was this conference in 1883 that laid the framework of the Indian Nation. Each nation sent to the Council of Chiefs at least one representative. If it was an extraordinarily large nation such as the Sioux, the bands within the nation could send chiefs once the council at large had agreed so by vote. All votes needed a two-thirds majority. These were safeguards to protect the smaller nations.

The Council had the power to declare war. It did not have the power to levy taxes, but since it was generally the custom to share with the poor and volunteer for community duties, taxes were not particularly important.

The Council did not have the power to deal with the internal problems of nations, unless it decided by vote that the problem presented imminent danger to other nations. A four-fifths vote was needed for this.

The Council did not have police powers. However, the presence of Dog Soldiers and other warrior societies guaranteed execution of Council decisions.

The Council granted the Wasichu Mormons one chief.

The war chiefs were elected by warrior societies, though a nation did not have to send a war chief if it did not want to. The Council of War Chiefs decided which societies would be responsible for defending which borders for how long. Chiefs were elected by their societies as usual, according to how successful they were and how many warriors they brought back alive. (This is one of the explanations of why They Fear His Horses did not mount a final, conclusive attack on Hayes. A chief who won victories at any cost was regarded a mentally ill man.)

The following year, Chief Taylor of Salt Lake City died in a fit. Wovoka was left as the leader of the Mormon Church and innovations came quickly. To the stricture against alcohol was added acceptance of peyote. Most of the Plains nations used it anyway, even some of the eastern ones like the Tuscarora. Peyote aided in visions and in the war against whiskey that American traders continued to try to market over the border.

Tavibo was raised to the level of Moroni in the Mormon hierarchy. Joseph Smith was declared to have Indian ancestry. Mormon himself was proclaimed to be a son of Wakon Tonka, the Great Mysterious One. Mormon's new job was as keeper of the Thunderbird.

As might be expected, a great number of the original Mormons packed up and left the Indian Nation. A surprising number, however, almost half, were impressed by Wovoka's monumental sincerity and remained true to their beliefs. With the Cherokee, they were instrumental in teaching the elements of plains farming to the nations and also in the founding of the agricultural universities.

With Wovoka leading the church, Sitting Bull, the Council of Chiefs, and Victorio, the War Chiefs, John Setter faded from Camp of the Nations, the town that had sprung up around the conference building. He retired to Sugar Hill in Mchweaming with a number of bright, young secretaries eager to learn the arts of foreign policy.

Sitting Bull was chief of the Nation until 1890 when he died. Under him, railroads were built from Camp of the Nations to every direction, like the spokes of a wheel, curving only to save the grounds of the buffalo. The Europeans were not able to establish the circle of build-tax-loan that they had in China, but they did welcome the gold and silver that came in a steady stream from the Indian Nation.

They Fear His Horses built something else. Every breakthrough in military technology was tested by his warriors. His Dog Soldiers were the first to be equipped with the Hotchkiss Gun, a gas-driven machine gun. Krupp nine-inchers replaced the Civil War howitzers. The raiding parties encouraged by the United States met a fate that sobered prospective successors. When They Fear His Horses became chief of the Nation, he left a military machine that naturally became the first with a serious air force.

Visitors without guns were welcomed. The Indians became a force in the arts, first as subjects and then as inspiration. Edgar Degas traveled to New Orleans to see his relatives; he could not resist traveling on to the Indian Nation where he stayed for two years painting Lakota, Crow, and Siksika women going about their daily chores. Other artists followed. Remington, Manet,

Pissarro, Cassatt, Gauguin (who never left), and, in modern days, Benton, Dali, and Riggs have all painted the Indian. It was not until Picasso that a painter acknowledged Indian art—Lakota pictographs, Chilkat and Navaho blankets, Iroquois false faces, Pueblo sand paintings, Maklak sculpture, Zuni jewelry—as the inspiration of his own. Pollack, Mondrian, and Moore were others to explore the intricacies of the Indian imagination.

The increasingly huge wood and steel tipis that dotted the plains were ignored by architects till Ludwig Mies van der Rohe made his belated visit in the 1930s. Oddly enough, besides adventure books, little was written about the Indian Nation until Jack London and Ernest Hemingway. Perhaps because of a lack of written tradition among the Indians, or the influence of John Setter, who said before he died, "The large personal library is the treasure of the intelligent idiot."

Or perhaps it was due to bad experiences like the one had by Friedrich Engels. Setter's old Washington friend, Morgan, published a book called *Ancient Society* in 1877 that excited Marx and led Engels to use Morgan's work as the basis for *The Origin of the Family, Private Property and the State* seven years later. It was all about the Iroquois and the constitution of the new Indian Nation. Engels rhapsodized, "And a wonderful constitution it is in all its childlike simplicity! No soldiers, no gendarmes or police, no nobles, kings, prefects, regents, or judges, no prisons, no lawsuits."

He couldn't wait until he visited this warriors' paradise. Tkachev's writings were no longer scoffed at in Marxist circles; Primitive Communism was all the rage. Traveling from Vera Cruz, Engels had the luck to meet both They Fear His Horses and John Setter. His excitement grew. Despite the fact that Indian government was secondary to traditions of communal living that stretched back for thousands of years, here was Communism

151

in the raw! Engels didn't know how raw. After filling notebooks about the lack of private property, the automatic sharing on the basis of "to each according to his needs," the apparent absolute liberty of all in camp, he joined a Dog Soldier patrol along the Texas border.

As if on cue, a party of Texas Rangers hunting Indian bounties attacked the patrol. Gall, the Lakota, was in charge of the Indians. He led the Rangers into a ravine, turned back, and cut them down before they could escape. Engels, his riding clothes tacky with sweat, fell from his horse onto the ground. When the Indians saw there was nothing the matter with him, they went about stripping the Texans of everything of value.

Engels dragged himself toward Gall, who was squatting over a dead body with his back turned. The theoretician called to Gall to get his attention and a drink of water. Gall heard him and turned to him. Engels felt his stomach leap like a rabbit and then gush through his mouth. Gall was eating the Texan's heart. Blood covered the lower half of his face, his hands, and his chest. The body with its gaping breast sprawled on a blanket of gore. Gall went on contentedly chewing.

The fact that Gall was only incorporating the dead man's bravery by eating his heart, an infrequent act but one still done by some older warriors at the time, was no explanation to Engels. He made a transatlantic dash back to London. The mere mention of Indians made him burp for the rest of his life.

To the United States, the main thing was that the Indian Nation had been labeled as Communist. If the United States has had one abiding passion since the 1870s, it has been its terror of Communism. Mistrust of the Indians grew until only the fact of the mechanized Dog Soldiers restrained an American attack. The Western United States was peculiarly obsessed with the Red Menace. When Congress set stricter immigration laws after the

Battle of Yellow Buttes, New York City's population was more than fifty percent foreign born. Most were German and Irish. The new immigrants from Italy and Middle Europe went where they were not discouraged, the relatively empty Pacific states. Hungry for property and wracked at the same time with wide family obligations and socialist yearnings, the new Americans helped create a wealthy, turbulent land. There was only one way they could assuage the suspicion of the entrenched authorities they found. That was to abjure forcefully the concepts of Communism and anarchism. So, through California, Oregon, Nevada, Washington, and Alaska, small but emotional purges were entertained. No settlement was too tiny not to have a radical to tar and feather. Hawaii had its first lynching in 1901.

Bells rang and militia ran to their armories when word came of the Russian Revolution in the Pacific states. Everyone agreed that the Bolshies would try to cross right over to Alaska with their red banners. When they didn't, everyone agreed that only vigilance had halted them. Confirmed in their hysteria, Western America proclaimed itself the bastion of democracy. They didn't need the Zimmermann Telegram to give them nightmares of unwashed Commies climbing over the ramparts of the bastion in hordes.

The telegram first fell into English hands on January 17, 1917, three years into the Great War. The United States had refrained from entering the battle because it had no love for the British. America had a worldwide fleet, however, and unlimited submarine warfare would push them onto the Allied side. A publisher turned decoder named de Grey broke the telegram sent in numerical groups by Zimmermann, the German Foreign Secretary, to Count von Bernstorff, the German Ambassador to the Indian Nation. It read:

"We intend to begin unrestricted submarine warfare on the

first of February . . . We make the Indian Nation a proposal of alliance on the following basis: make war together, make peace together, generous financial assistance, and an understanding on our part that the Indian Nation regain its lost territory of California, Nevada, Washington, and Oregon . . . You will inform the chief of the Nation of the above most secretly as soon as the outbreak of war with the United States is certain, and add the suggestion that he should, on his own initiative, invite Japan to immediate adherence and at the same time mediate between Japan and ourselves. . . . Zimmermann."

The threat was not from the north, not even from white men, but from east and west and by yellow and red men! The United States threw its weight with England and France without a week's delay. Horses and cars moved back and forth like eyes waiting for the Indians to make their attack along some remote stretch of the border.

There was no attack, of course. The proposal was infantile in its credulity. Indians also remembered the Kaiser as the man who circulated around the Berlin embassies a painting he commissioned. The painting, after his own sketch, showed a rabid Wovoka riding a Thunderbird over the burning cities of America and Europe. At his sides were a Chinese and a Japanese, each drooling with lust as the unholy trio approached a band of poorly clad ladies signifying the white nations. An archangel acting as observer shouted, "People of the white race, guard your most precious possessions!" Wilhelm was no favorite of the object of his crude advance.

Relations between the Indian Nation and Japan were something else. They Fear His Horses stepped down as chief of the Nation in 1910 when he instituted five-year terms for the highest position in the country. By then, Japanese military and trading missions were commonplace on the prairies. The first ironworks in the crescent-shaped city of the Tsitsistas was built with Japanese advisors. This friendship between the Indians and America's foremost rival in the Pacific was a special threat in the minds of Sacramento and Washington. Zimmermann's delusion was shared just enough for the United States to enter into the Agreement of Sacramento in June 1918. For the first time the US had formally recognized the Indian Nation. As if his work had finally been done, Where the Sun Goes, a Mandan also known as John Setter, died that summer at the age of ninety, full of honors. His body was cremated and the ashes scattered in the wind, according to his wish.

The '20s passed in a rush for the United States. Samoa became part of the American empire as a prize of war and its development spurred speculation in the Pacific; the British had offered Bermuda and Jamaica as inducements for the US to fight and these acquisitions boosted banks in the eastern states. The world had never seen the like of America's maritime. Even President Coolidge suffered the indignity of campaigning in a sailor's cap. Prospective presidents like Franklin Roosevelt made service in the Department of the Navy part of their background. In the Indian Nation, without a fleet or empire, progress seemed at a standstill. Capital growth was one hundredth of its neighbor's as miners spent half their time rehabilitating mines amid ceremonies of regret to the Earth Mother. Even oil wells were ringed with sacred sage to atone for their use. Families continued to make their own clothes and gain their own food by hunting and farming, the latter in a slow, careful way so as not to kill the grassland.

"They cannot change" the *National Geographic* picture caption said to describe an Indian pilot hanging his medicine pouch in the cockpit of a plane. The article went on to deplore the fact that despite their accomplishments, the Indians still had not grasped the benefits of Western civilization. Their logic was different, their colors, their emotions, their needs, even their definition of what was real or unreal was inferior. Americans felt as a teacher might with a slow learner.

Yet a few years later when the second Great Depression came, when dust devils swirled from Texas to South Carolina and savings vanished in invisible winds, America looked to the Indian Nation with bald envy. There the land was fertile, unravaged. The ignorant savages living on it were practically unaware of the worldwide financial crisis since their economy was based on merely serving their wants. Banks were nonexistent because the idea of hoarding money was repugnant. Factories were started as a common venture between the people of a nation when the idea had been fully discussed and a vote taken. And factories were generally only for the use of other Indians. The concept of faraway peoples as markets and themselves as the providers of raw materials was never a popular one. The end result was, as Joseph Kennedy put it, that "the Indians are too damn dumb to suffer the consequences of modern capital investment."

There was some effort, particularly by Louisiana Governor Huey Long, to provoke a war with the Indian Nation as a way of providing employment for the millions of men without jobs. If Hoover, the Asian mining expert, had still been in the White House, Long might have succeeded. The new president was Franklin Roosevelt, a forceful personality who declared that "Long's advice on unemployment makes him the most dangerous man in America." Roosevelt's remark was not thoroughly idealistic; Charles Lindberg had reported to him that the Indian Air Force was as mighty as the Luftwaffe. America satisfied itself with civilian, not military, make-work while President Roosevelt launched a "Good Neighbor Policy" with the Inde Chief of the Nation, Francisco. For the first time an American president was invited to Camp of the Nations, where a Sun Dance was held in his honor. "It's very much like a Virginia Reel, I would say," he reported to America in a fireside chat, "except for the scalps, of course."

On December 7, 1941, the era of good feeling came to an end. Imperialist Japan was sweeping through America's Pacific states toward California. Hirohito demanded Indian support the same hour Roosevelt did. The chief of the Indian Nation at this moment was the Tsitsistas Water Knife, a tall, heavy man much like a brown Washington, slow and certain in his thoughts. Crews at a hundred Indian air terminals rolled their planes onto the runways.

"If we joined the Japanese, what would you say?" he asked his War Chief Buffalo Rider, a Lenape.

"The Germans have won in Europe unless they run out of gasoline. The Japanese have control of the Pacific. With our oil and planes, it would be very difficult for the English or the Americans to hold out for long," Buffalo Rider said. He was young with hair that reached to his waist, typical of most of the lean officers of the army.

"You don't sound enthusiastic," Water Knife said. It was right for a warrior to be modest, but the Lenape was unusually somber.

"I'm not. An hour ago I possibly would have given you a different answer, that we were ready and eager to attack with the Japanese. You must remember that I have many Japanese friends. But in the meantime I have recalled the first duty of a war chief: to save the lives of as many of his men as he can. I would be killing many Indians if I advised a declaration of war, wouldn't I? We would get nothing but revenge and it's not worth it, I suppose."

"Revenge for what?" Water Knife asked.

The question stopped Buffalo Rider. He thought for a minute, raised his hands, and smiled.

Water Knife spoke with President Roosevelt that evening. The Indian Nation would not go to war for either side, he said. It would retaliate against any nation that trespassed its borders. When Roosevelt said that this was support for the Japanese, Water Knife said that it was the opposite. It meant that a Japanese invasion of the Western US would automatically fail in its main purpose, since to get at the rest of its enemy it would have to cross a hostile Indian Nation. As proof of its good intentions, the Indians would institute an oil embargo to all belligerents, a move that would adversely affect only the Axis powers; it was also the same move the United States made when it was a neutral. He would go no further than that. There was a long silence on the other end of the phone and then the president said, "Dandy."

There was no Japanese invasion and there was no Axis victory. Instead, there was a United Nations, with the United States getting a vote for each of its two sections. It was not the only landmark for the Western US. The Twentieth Amendment to the Constitution created a rotation of the presidency between the East and West every four years. By now the Pacific states embraced the Carolina Islands, Okinawa, and Midway. When South Korea was invaded by North Korean Communists, there was no hesitation in rushing to its defense with the rest of the UN not far behind.

The Indian Nation was not a member of the UN. The vote over whether to join or not was discussed in all the camps of the country, from Grey Fox's River in the land of the Lakota to Goy-ya-thle's Rifle in the mesas of the Inde, and it was decided that Indians had no business going off to die in someone else's quarrels far away, which they saw as one of the obligations of membership. It was something run by Wasichu and how could they presume to understand Wasichu quarrels? Americans were always saying that Indians were crazy because they didn't have states, and Indians asked why should they have states? This is where one nation lives and that is where another nation lives. It was as simple as that.

The refusal of the Indian Nation to join the United Nations cooled relations with the US again. Soviet Russia was not happy, either, that it could not persuade the Indians to join on their side. Each power glared at the Indians and waved its atomic bombs menacingly. In October 1952, Chief of the Nation Orange Moon called together news correspondents in the auditorium of the new forty-story tipi in the capital. The phlegmatic Maklak told them that Indian scientists had devised their own atomic bomb.

The reporters went into shock. When had the bomb been tested? they asked. It hadn't been, Orange Moon said. When would it be tested? Orange Moon raised his eyebrows. Never, he said. Who would release a hideous thing like this just to see if it worked? The Mother Earth was a far too precious spirit for that.

Teletype messages came quickly from Washington, Moscow, and London. All of them demanded that the bomb be tested so that they would know if Orange Moon was telling the truth. He said that his scientists told him that it would work and that was enough for him. More messages came, offering test sites if the Indians refused to set it off on their own land. Orange Moon recoiled, saying that he would not be responsible for despoiling other people's land. The Indians had the bomb and that was the end of it. For months after, newspapers around the world made fun of the Indians' paper bomb but in the end they found themselves believing in it all the same.

The bomb was like the Indians in a way.

As Western civilization, people's democratic republics, the Third World, gross national products, per capita income, inflation, and the Free World progressed to their fitful conclusion, the Indians were like some barely believable affront. Despite all the proofs of Twentieth Century Man, those by which he measured himself and found himself not wanting, the Indians existed and had existed for almost a century as a nation. It had had no wars since its liberation, no mass depressions economically or spiritually, never shown signs of intellectual discontent. The reason was obvious. It had chosen stagnation over progress. Still, it was a little like Cro-Magnon Man discovering an island of Neanderthals living quite happily away in its midst. The US and the rest of the world were forced to believe it, but they didn't like it.

"Your history has led you into the sea like evolution in reverse. You end up on the border of Asia and feel you must fight there. Not rational but logical. Otherwise, you never would have fought the Vietnamese, I assume, if the Philippines were not a state. You win and you try to come home to this continent. Perhaps you even meant to be peaceful, but you are so infected with violence that you can kill our chief and blame us for it. Now you are willing to destroy part of this land to win all of it. Why? Because you and the Soviets have made your own kind of peace where you allow each other to kill as long as it is in a sphere of influence. The Russians slaughter Czechs and Chinese. It is only fair that you kill Indians. The advantage you have over us is that you can lose so many people without missing them. Also, that every chief since Orange Moon has sworn that the Indian Nation will never use its atomic weapons unless they have already been used in an attack on us.

"My latest communication with Camp of the Nations has changed that. The new chief will use his discretion in employing nuclear weapons any time he feels that the integrity of the Indian Nation is in jeopardy. He feels that this position will aid in the successful conclusion of these talks since it will disarm those extremists who might push for a preventive strike against Indian forces."

The line of faces on the other side of the table had been registering shock since Holds Eagles started. For a moment none of them said a word as the stenographers tapped out the last sentence of the opening statement. It was their twentieth meeting, and the United States had come prepared with an ultimatum for an Indian withdrawal from the northern territories. That was out the window now.

"That's against your religion," Nielson blurted out. "You're not supposed to harm the Mother Earth."

"There's been a new Revelation," Holds Eagles said.

Harry Moore pursed his lips. The two Indians waited for a reply that was reluctant to come. The well-oiled table reflected the two miniature flags, one with fifty-five stars and thirteen stripes in red, white, and blue, the other a red sun with a white ring set on a green field.

"I suggest that we recess and discuss the implications of the statement of the Indian government," Moore said.

Actually, it was the Indians who left, escorted to their car by the Press Aide as Nielson and his staff slumped around the table.

"Huh. What ever happened to sweetness and light? He came on pretty strong today," a justice man said.

"Maybe he blew it. Let's check out what he said with the Council of Chiefs and see whether they go along this time," the navy chief said and smacked his hands together. He went out the door enthusiastically.

"Harry," the president said.

"Yes?"

"Harry, things haven't been going the way you said they would. Nothing's gone right. Did you see the TV yesterday, the demonstrations in New York, even in Sacramento?"

"We have to act fast, I agree, Mr. President."

A security man coughed and made for the door.

"Wait," Nielson said. It was an order, something unusual for the president. "I want everyone to hear this. Harry, you said that we could pull this thing off with practically no damage. They'd never get a missile in the air, you said. I don't consider that probable now if what Holds Eagles says is the truth. I may be a fool, but I am also the president. I'm not going to see half the United States blown off the map to find out whether you're right. Perhaps I've spent most of my life on the islands and growing roses in Pasadena, but I am not going down in history as the idiot who ruined the greatest nation on earth. Do you read me, Harry?"

"Yes, Mr. President."

"I'm beginning to smell something, too, Harry."

The attorney general's face turned an unaccustomed red. "I don't understand, Mr. President. You're letting the United States be threatened by a messenger boy. There's no reason to back down from our original plan. We went all through this before. We've got the largest military force in the world along with the largest military budget. That's got to be justified somewhere. For the first time the Indians not only have no European allies to help them out, but we've got a go-ahead from the Russians. This is the biggest opportunity the United States has had in a hundred years. Unless you welcome a hundred years of Americans—five hundred million of them—squeezed like cattle against the seacoasts so that some primitives can play Stone Age. Nobody ever said being president was nice."

"Actually, it's a decision that many presidents have had to make in the past," a staffer on leave from Harvard said. "Washington, Jackson, Harrison, Adams, Grant, all had this same argument with the same goal in mind—secure borders."

"I've heard all this before," the president said. "By the way, you left out Hayes. When you've got some word from the Indian Council, let me know. Until then, this meeting is adjourned."

President Nielson rode the small elevator up to the living quarters in the East Wing. A gallery of predecessors looked down from their frames as he walked down the hall shaking his head. At the end of the corridor was a gift from the Anheuser-Busch Company, a painting of Custer's Last Stand, with the general aiming his gun somewhere over Nielson's left shoulder. It reminded him that of all the men on his side of the negotiating table, he was the only one who had ever fought hand to hand with brown guerrillas. He was almost a throwback in that way. Custer looked glorious alone on his knoll surrounded by a thousand Indians. But it wasn't that way. It was odd, but he felt that Holds Eagles was the only other man in the room who knew that. It wasn't that way at all.

The admiral reported to the attorney general first. The Council had told UPI that it already knew of the statement made by its representative at the bargaining table and that it had their full authorization.

"Did they name the new chief of the Nation?" Moore asked.

"Nope. It was just a statement by them. I can tell you that television vans are pulling up in front of the White House so the word is out. Fish or cut bait. Bad time for the president to start having second thoughts. What about that idea you've been talking about?"

"Leave it to me," Moore said.

In the last month Liz Carney had come alive. When the black car with diplomatic plates stopped at the corner of the National Press Building, she glowed like a schoolgirl. She got in back with Holds Eagles. Two Dog Soldiers were in front.

"Let's go to my place and you can tell me all about it," she suggested.

"Afraid not," he said. "Things are popping now. I just wanted to talk to you for a second, then I've got to get back to the embassy."

She looked at the grim DS and then at the guns clipped to the panel. "I can see. It's hit the fan at the White House, I can tell you that. Leak about a big fight after you left. Are you trying to tell me something now?"

"Yes."

"Like I'm not going to see you for a while, right?"

"I'm sorry. I can drop you off at your place, but I have to get back."

"Thanks. Well, it was nice while it lasted. It couldn't go on forever. Before I break down and make a fool of myself, have you got a funny story to take my mind off things?"

"Funny story?" He watched a solid color car with two men make a U-turn and trail the limousine sedately.

"A true one. A true funny story," Liz said.

"True funny. Let's see. Names, you like stories about Indian names. How about one of those?"

"Fine."

"This is true. A while back there was a Lakota who was a very mean guy. Had the dirtiest tipi, the scrawniest horses, gave as little to the poor as he could, and when he gave a feast it was with the skinniest old bulls he could find. People went away as hungry as they came. He was a very nasty guy and his name was Johnny Farts When He Eats."

Her sniffling stopped. "You're kidding."

"No. Cross my heart. He didn't like it, either, but that was his name, and for a very good reason. He did. You can understand that people laughed at Johnny Farts When He Eats, and it was very difficult for him to impress anyone. Finally, he got fed up. He went to his camp council and asked that his name be changed. They told him he would have to follow the custom, which was that the council would meet for three days, and during that time they would decide on a new name for Johnny Farts When He Eats. He would have to feast the camp while the council was in session. They warned him that it had better be a good feast with fat calves and turkeys, and he agreed. So the council came together while Johnny went off in his beat-up station wagon to buy food. Sure enough, Johnny came back and feasted the camp on the thinnest, oldest, most meatless bulls anyone had ever seen, while Johnny stood around proud that he had fooled the council. He was not a popular man. All the same, he went to the council when the three days were up and asked what his new name was. They told him that they had changed their minds; they weren't going to give him one. Johnny had a fit. He jumped up and down screaming that he had done as they asked and feasted everyone in the camp and said he would go on screaming until they fulfilled their part of the bargain.

"They saw that he was serious and they did not want to cause a scene so they said, 'Okay, give us one more day and we promise we will give you a new name.' They talked it over all night and the next morning they called Johnny up before the whole camp. From hence forward, he was to be known as Johnny Does Not Fart When He Eats. True story."

One of the Dog Soldiers shook silently in subterranean laughs. Liz laughed aloud. "You're kidding; you made it up," she said.

"True. Ask any man here."

"Oh. You've got me crying the other way now. Wait a second." She checked her face in the mirror. Holds Eagles saw the car in back slow down a bit, warily. "Now I've got something for you. My years as a reporter have not been wasted. I have figured something out. Namely, who the new chief of the Nation is."

The Dog Soldier in the front seat was definitely not laughing.

"Who?" Holds Eagles asked.

"Why, you, of course," she said with pride. "It's as simple as ABC. There aren't any instantaneous secret communications between your embassy and the Council back home. That's a front. All they do is agree generally with everything you say no matter how wild it is, even about there being a new chief back there. It's the old shell game, keeping the eye on one hand while the other hand does all the work. You're no diplomat, you're the real thing, the McCoy."

Holds Eagles smiled. "Is that what you think? I'm very complimented."

"It's obvious as can be once somebody stops thinking about it the other way. It's the only way things make sense."

The limousine drove up a familiar street. "Here's your house," Holds Eagles said. They parked as the other car stopped at the corner. "It's a crazy theory."

"I know," Liz said. "So I'll keep it to myself until we meet again. Goodbye."

She got out of the car and rushed to the house. Holds Eagles waited until she was inside and then the limousine pulled away. The car at the corner did the same.

The limousine passed through Georgetown with its shadow. The Dog Soldier at the wheel sped up and slowed down experimentally, watching the plain sedan ape his actions. When they got to one of the wide avenues leading back to the city, the driver said, "There are two now. Gaining on us."

"Don't try to lose them. Stay with the traffic," Holds Eagles said.

A third and a fourth car joined them in front. All of them

were unmarked sedans with a pair of men. The Dog Soldier not driving took a submachine gun from under the seat. Holds Eagles put a small, heavy box on his lap and wondered if the pistols inside could still shoot.

"They've got radios. There are some more cars ahead," the driver said. Without waiting for an order, he swerved the limousine into a side street and accelerated down it.

The Indians raced onto the next avenue they found. A police car started after them, saw the diplomatic plates, and stopped with a curse. They were in Washington now, approaching the wide mall that runs from the Hill to the Washington Monument.

"Made it," the driver said with a grin. "Good medicine."

A plain sedan coming the other way suddenly turned into their path, pinning the limousine to a light pole. Two more sedans came up from behind. The Dog Soldier at the wheel was dead, his head halfway through the windshield. Holds Eagles stumbled out the back, the box in his hand. Two men with guns out were running toward him.

The other Dog Soldier came out of the front, his forehead red with blood. He cut down the first two men with the submachine gun and whirled on his knees to shoot the rest. He got all but the last one before he fell forward, his long black hair covering his face.

Holds Eagles was running over the mall. He didn't look back, just changed his direction slightly every few feet. On top of the needle in honor of George Washington, tourists peeked through the narrow gun slot windows and pointed at the man dashing crazily over the ground and the men following him. Holds Eagles felt a tug on his leather shirt and saw the earth in front of him shoot up.

Cars stopped in front of the monument and men started running out of them. He looked behind and saw a sedan jerk up onto the ground and start after him, dodging through the men already following.

Holds Eagles made it first. The car lurched to a halt as he melted into the crowd. He pushed his way to a group of teenagers holding balloons in the line. They were dressed in leather jackets, the same as his.

"Run, the cops are out to bust you!" he said.

They didn't wait to be told twice. There were four of them and each ran in a different direction. A merry-go-round stopped and its load of children took the long step down to their mothers. One stood unclaimed, looking around. Holds Eagles took the boy's hand and said, "Your mommy asked me to take you for some ice cream." The boy's eyes widened with anticipation and he kept his mouth shut. Holds Eagles slipped his fringed jacket off as he and the child walked casually down the sidewalk. The men from the cars were rounding up the scared teenagers quietly, professionally.

"My mommy didn't bring me; my daddy brought me," the boy said when they were halfway down the block. He seemed to approve of conspiracy.

The father appeared, yelling and shouting as he came from the merry-go-round. Holds Eagles gave the boy a pat on the bottom and sent him back, then walked briskly to a line forming in front of a huge, castle-like building.

"Are you a member of the group?" a white-haired lady with glasses asked him.

"Yes, but I lost my identification badge," Holds Eagles said.

"Well then, just follow me," she said pleasantly, "and we can get you another badge later."

A guide met them inside, leading them under a number of kite-like flying machines and through a number of other tour groups. The tourists saw rockets and locomotives and early

American figures in wax and a bottled brain that was heavier than Daniel Webster's.

By the merry-go-round, the gray sedans had parked in a row. A limousine the same color joined the end and the agents in charge ran down to it.

"We've lost him. A guy said he walked off with his kid. The kid's back. We're still looking for the Indian, though."

The colorless man in the back of the car muttered a few words. Two of the sedans took off toward Georgetown.

The attorney general arrived at the White House at suppertime. He bustled in from the underground car garage with his hand full of papers.

"Please excuse me, Mr. President, for bursting in on you like this," he said as he came into the president's office. "I know you're eating."

"Eating?" Nielson said and looked around. "I don't see any food. Sit down."

"This is important," the attorney general said. "Too important for the phone. Remember I told you that the Indian Holds Eagles was seeing the TV reporter Liz Carney socially? I've just come from her house. She's been murdered, mutilated. It happened a little more than an hour ago. The Indian did it. These are the police reports."

He placed the papers in front of the president carefully. Nielson was amazed.

"He was seen entering with her and leaving alone with his clothes stained. Plenty of witnesses," the Attorney General said. "Of course, you know what this does to the talks."

"I am shocked. But these reports are quite complete. Very," he said as he sifted through them.

"My men helped out. I'm afraid the news has already leaked out; we were too late for that."

President Nielson leaned back in his chair and gave Moore the benefit of an appreciative smile. "I'm sure you did your best, Harry. There's no doubt in your mind."

"Absolutely none. I have some other news too, sir. Holds Eagles is actually the new chief of the Nation. I had my first hunch on that after this morning's meeting. I didn't want to say anything until I'd checked it out. I've done that now. We've got him right in our hands."

"You're right," Nielson said. He rose from his chair and started pacing the room. "Quite right. By the way, Harry, have you ever taken a good look at this office, some of the mementoes I have here?"

"Mr. President. . . ."

"Bear with me. Look, here's one of the first .45's used in the Philippines for the Huk. a Samoan war shield here. President Dewey's receipt of the order that sent him to Manila. All these footsteps, figurative of course, of our progress through the oceans as the American Nation spread its power. A samurai sword from Tarawa. A musket ball from Jamaica. Probably fired by a pirate. My own sea desk. It's history, Harry, right here."

"I understand, Mr. President, but time is pressing."

"I know. And look at this. Perhaps the greatest souvenir this country has ever seen." He took a box from the top of his desk and opened it. Set in velvet were two old, highly polished handguns. "Self-cocking, double-action Irish Constabulary pistols. Real pearl handles. Custer's guns, Harry, imagine that. The ones he went down with."

The attorney general said nothing.

"The greatest historical treasure in the Indian Nation, given to me as a token of esteem by Chief Holds Eagles at the same time you have him off killing someone, witnesses and all. How do you explain that, Harry?"

Holds Eagles walked in through a side door. He was tempted to kill the grey man, as he had been when he first heard the accusation through the door. But he couldn't; all his training had been to ignore filth. By an act of concentration, he blotted Moore from the room.

The president was enjoying himself. "The chief was coming here to give me the present as a purely private matter when some of your men ran into him on the mall. He phoned from the Smithsonian and I had a White House car go around and pick him up. We've been talking. He informed me of his true status in the Indian Nation. Means you tried to assassinate a head of state and almost makes me wonder what happened with Buffalo Rider. As your closest friend and adviser, Harry, let me tell you. You're in trouble."

The talks between the Indian Nation and the United States resumed two weeks later. Each side of the table was fully staffed.

The president opened for the United States.

"Although troops have been withdrawn from the borders," he said, "this does not mean that my government feels any less urgency in rectifying those borders. The next hundred years will see vast changes on the continent we share. We must meet the challenges of those changes together. We must change, too."

Afterward, the president and Holds Eagles went for a walk outside. To the east, they could see the American side of the border, marked by a blue haze that floated over a small factory town. Where they were, the grass stretched away to the horizon marked only by an occasional butte and the shining aluminum tipi the conference was held in. Indians and Americans could be seen mixing together, smoking.

The two leaders made an odd pair. Nielson was in a formal black suit with a shirt collar that seemed too tight for his neck. His head bobbed up and down as they strolled. Holds Eagles was in white, fringed buckskin with a quill chest. His hair was growing again and he wore it in a simple headband.

"I was very impressed with what you had to say about changing," he told the president. "You're completely right."

As Nielson stared at the clean horizon line of green against blue, Holds Eagles undid a pouch of thin paper and tobacco. He let a seed pod fall and rolled the cigarette in sure, unhurried motions.

Nielson pulled out a lighter and lit the cigarette for Holds Eagles, watching as the chief sucked the sweet smoke in deeply.

"Hey," the president asked, "could you make one for me?"

The Indians Won